TAINTED TRUFFLE
TREACHERY

TAINTED TRUFFLE TREACHERY

REG RAWLINS, PSYCHIC INVESTIGATOR
BOOK TWENTY

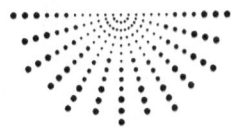

P.D. WORKMAN

 **PD WORKMAN**

ISBN: 9781774685808 (KDP Paperback)
ISBN: 9781774685815 (KDP Hardcover)
ISBN: 9781774685839 (Large Print)
ISBN: 9781774685846 (Lulu Paperback)
ISBN: 9781774685822 (ePub)
ISBN: 9781774685853 (Accessible Audio)

ALSO BY P. D. WORKMAN

FIND MORE BOOKS AT PDWORKMAN.COM

MYSTERY/SUSPENSE:

Reg Rawlins, Psychic Detective
Paranormal Mystery & Adventure
What the Cat Knew
A Psychic with Catitude
A Catastrophic Theft
Night of Nine Tails
The Immortal's Key
Yule's Sinister Spell
Fairy Blade Unmade
Web of Nightmares
A Whisker's Breadth
Skunk Man Swamp
Magic Ain't A Game
Without Foresight
Careful of Thy Wishes
Time to Your Elf
Undiscovered Tomb
Missing Powers
Thrice Spared
Cloaked Campaign
Sleepwalker's Sanctuary
Cat Tales in the Swamp (Short Story)

Tainted Truffle Treachery (Coming Soon)

A Fowl Play on Christmas Day (Christmas crossover story)

Lunar Lies (Coming Soon)

Zachary Goldman Mysteries

Private Investigator

She Wore Mourning

His Hands Were Quiet

She Was Dying Anyway

He Was Walking Alone

They Thought He was Safe

He Was Not There

Her Work Was Everything

She Told a Lie

He Never Forgot

She Was At Risk

He Drowned in Memory

Their Walls Were Empty

They Came for Him

They Sought Vengeance

She Was Their Target

His Fear Was Real

Stand Alone Suspense Novels

Looking Over Your Shoulder

Lion Within

Pursued by the Past

In the Tick of Time

Loose the Dogs

AND MORE AT PDWORKMAN.COM

To faithful friends
who aren't always normal

CHAPTER ONE

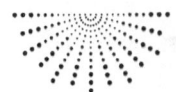

*R*eg was happy to be home. Going to the Everglades for a few days to visit Etienne and his new wife, Ilka, had been a nice diversion and helped her to get her mind off of recent events in Black Sands. Still, it was always nice to get home again. She was happy to have a home to go to after so many years of being shuttled from one place to another every few months. She had been in Black Sands for over a year. A lot had happened during that time, and it was home now. The little guest cottage she had rented from Sarah on her first day in Black Sands had become her sanctuary and home base. She ate and slept there, ran her psychic business holding readings and seances there and, of course, there was Starlight.

She put down the cat carrier and let out the black and white tuxedo cat with a white splash on his forehead. Starlight took his time oozing out of the carrier, arching his back, and then elongating all his muscles, vibrating with the joy of the stretch. Reg reached down and scratched his ears and then along his back, hoping it would help to work out any fatigue or soreness from their trip. She wished someone would come and give *her* a back rub and massage. It wasn't like she'd been traveling all day, but the three-legged trip—first on donkey, then airboat, and then car—had seemed very long.

Of course, Corvin would be happy to get a call from her to massage her sore body, but he wouldn't stop there. She would feel good for a while, but he would strip her of her powers, which she knew from sad experience was not something she could tolerate. She would go crazy with the silence in her own head. She was too used to the other voices there, always vying for her attention, and didn't know how normal people lived with the silence.

Reg let out a noisy sigh at the thought of Corvin. She had expected the phone to ring as soon as she got in the door, Corvin asking if she were home and when he could see her. Having shared magic, memories, and thoughts with her before, he had an uncanny sense of where she was and what she was doing. She could never quite keep him out of her head.

He had told her he had some news she would be interested in. Something that he couldn't tell her over the phone—though that was probably just a ruse. He wanted a chance to see her face to face, just as he always did, so that he might get the opportunity to seduce her and take away her gifts.

But his words echoed in her mind. "I have a job for you. Something you're going to want to do."

A job? What would Corvin need her to do for him? He was very powerful and grew stronger all the time. She had to be careful of him, to always be aware that today he might be stronger than yesterday and that what had worked before would not necessarily work again.

She would find out tomorrow. She had managed to put him off for a day, which was probably why he hadn't phoned the minute she walked in the door. Then she and the handsome warlock would sit across from each other at the restaurant of their choosing, and he would tell her about... whatever it was he wanted her to look into. Some little thing that he had made up to get her interest. A lost ring. A haunting. A friend who wanted a psychic to do readings at her birthday party.

It wasn't going to be anything earth-shattering. She was sure of that.

* * *

Starlight marched directly to his bowl. It was, of course, empty. They had been away from the house for several days and she had not left food out for him.

He put his ears back in a grumpy cat scowl and narrowed his mismatched blue and green eyes at her.

"I'm sorry, Your Majesty," Reg told him, rolling her eyes. "I'm sorry that food doesn't instantly appear in your dish the second we walk in the door. I think you can wait a few minutes while I put down my bags and splash some water on my face."

Starlight gave a short yowl, which indicated he would not be happy to wait for Reg to take care of her own physical needs while he waited.

"At least you could curl up and go to sleep in your carrier on the way home," Reg pointed out. And, of course, the carrier was lined with a soft blanket for his comfort. "You're not the one who had to sit on a donkey. And those hard boat chairs."

He did not seem sympathetic. Reg grabbed the plastic box of dry kibble and trickled a little into Starlight's bowl. He stared at her, waiting for the good stuff.

"That will hold you for now," Reg assured him, and walked by him to put her suitcase in her bedroom and take care of other matters.

When she returned to the kitchen, he was still sitting in front of his food dish, looking offended that she had only offered him dry kibble.

"You're spoiled, you know that?" Reg asked as she opened the door to the fridge and started rummaging through the plastic bowls to find some tuna or stew that he would enjoy. "First, you insist on coming with me to the Everglades—and I told you it was a swamp, so you can't complain if you got your paws a little wet— when you could have been nice and comfortable at home with

Sarah looking after you. You're the one who decided to go galli-vanting around with the panther while I was visiting with Etienne and Ilka. I don't know what you guys got into, but if you have an upset stomach or ticks, that's your own fault, not mine. You're the one who insisted."

Starlight just stared at his bowl, unmoving.

Reg got the distinct feeling that he was trying to train her to serve him properly, and he could do without the constant babble. She looked at him and raised an eyebrow.

"Really?"

He just looked at her, long-suffering, waiting for her to finally get around to putting something edible into his food dish.

Reg picked it up and added a couple of generous spoonfuls of tuna casserole, then put it on the floor in front of him. Starlight pushed her hand out of the way as he lunged forward to attack the tuna, poor starved cat that he was. His rumbling purr filled the room, and Reg couldn't feel too annoyed at him. The purr was soothing and assured her that she had done what she was supposed to.

A positive reinforcement for performing the expected behavior, she supposed. All part of her training.

Humans took a long time to train.

CHAPTER TWO

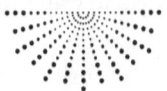

$\mathcal{E}$tienne and Ilka had been diligent in providing Reg with everything she needed while visiting them in their remote Everglades cabin. But all of the comforts of someone else's home couldn't replicate the feeling of falling into her own bed at the end of her workday, pulling up her sheets, and going to sleep. The bed was the right height and softness, not a hulking great thing she felt like a child climbing into. She couldn't deny that her bed in the cabin had been comfortable, but it had not been *right*.

She slept well. She did not have any nightmares. She actually woke up in the morning feeling well-rested and refreshed. Exactly how she should feel after a holiday.

She could hear someone moving around the house and knew without seeing that it was Sarah. Firstly, because Sarah was the only one who had a key and could get past the protective wards that she and Reg had set to ensure that Corvin couldn't walk into the cottage. Or anyone else who intended her harm. Also because Starlight had left the bedroom at the first stirrings of sound and there was no indication that he had attacked the intruder. Starlight was very territorial and, if someone who was a threat entered the cottage, he wouldn't hesitate to shred their lower limbs. He wasn't yowling for his breakfast, either, so Sarah had fed him.

For a while, she just luxuriated in the lazy morning warmth of her bed. What could be better? When she got up, she would have a good cup of coffee, check her planner schedule to see if Sarah had written in any new appointments for her, and just relax while she started the day at a nice, slow pace.

Sarah hung around longer than Reg expected, but she didn't poke her head in to tell Reg it was time to get up. Reg heard her leave the cottage and decided it was time. She just didn't want to have to deal with company before she saw Corvin. And if Sarah sensed that she was planning to visit Corvin… the old witch would not be happy with her, that was for sure.

When Reg got out to the kitchen and front room, Starlight was sitting on the back of the couch, watching birds out the window. He turned his head to look at Reg and made a small, satisfied noise of greeting. Sarah's feeding Starlight before Reg got up eliminated the need for the dance around a howling, rubbing cat doing his best to trip her up and insisting that he needed to be taken care of before she'd even had one shot of caffeine. It was the perfect morning.

The new coffee maker was already cued up and ready to go. All Reg had to do was push one button, and the dark, fragrant coffee started to fill her mug. Reg breathed in the high-octane fumes, ready to enjoy her liquid breakfast.

And then the phone rang.

Of course.

And it was Corvin.

Of course.

Reg looked at his name and picture on the screen of her phone and didn't answer it immediately. She waited for her coffee cup to be filled, then picked it up and carried it over to the couch, where she sat with her feet curled up under her, within petting distance of Starlight. By this time, her phone had stopped ringing but, before Reg could tap the screen to call Corvin back, it was ringing again. Reg swiped to accept the call and left it on the coffee table in speaker mode.

She took a sip of the scalding hot coffee before saying anything.

"Reg, are you there?" Corvin asked, sounding confused and irritated.

"Yeah. Just got to get some coffee in me."

She expected to hear his usual low, sexy chuckle and for him to make some comment about how late she had slept in. But he didn't. Reg took another sip of coffee, then reached out her senses toward him, curious about the lack of banter.

He was serious. Maybe not angry, but close to it. Not in any mood for Reg to be lighthearted or teasing. Definitely not the usual state of affairs.

"What's going on?" she asked him.

"We'll discuss that when we get together. Which I am hoping is before too long."

"Well… I *just* got up."

"Maybe we could meet for a donut. Or whatever other sugary confection grabs your fancy. Or one of those dreadful coffee-choco-late-caramel-cinnamon-whatever drinks you like so much at The Witches' Brew."

"I thought we could do a late lunch or early dinner. I'm not really ready to start into anything I have to think about this morning."

"It won't be morning much longer."

"Which is why I suggested lunch instead of breakfast."

Corvin gave an exasperated sigh. "When is the earliest you could drag yourself out of your lazy morning routine to meet me?"

"I'm not lazy. I was up late."

He knew that she was normally up into the small hours of the morning dealing with seances or other readings. That was why she slept so late in the morning, not because she was lazy. Reg's foster moms had always criticized her for being lazy, but Reg couldn't help the fact that her brain was built to stay up late and not fully engage until late morning or early afternoon.

Corvin didn't have to know that she hadn't actually had any readings the night before and had gone to bed early, considering her usual schedule. She *was* being lazy. But that was the only way to start the morning after a vacation. The only right way.

7

"When, Reg?" he asked impatiently.

"Late lunch or early dinner," she repeated evenly.

"So... one o'clock?"

"One thirty," Reg negotiated, without even looking at the clock to see what time it was. She did not want to go with his first suggestion. She needed to show him that she had a mind of her own.

Though it wasn't like he didn't already know that she had her own ideas about things. She hadn't exactly cooperated with him in the past. Except on a few occasions, which she usually regretted.

"One thirty, then," Corvin said sternly. "Where do you want to meet? The usual?"

"The Crystal Bowl," Reg confirmed. It had been a while since they had been to his private club, and she didn't want him to think that the club was "the usual." She didn't have any intention of going back *there*.

"Good," Corvin agreed, not arguing with her that he would prefer the club's privacy, as he often did.

His behavior was certainly different from usual. Did he have something really serious on his mind? He'd tried to emphasize that in his previous call, but Reg was too suspicious to believe everything he said. Not even most of it.

"Don't be late," Corvin growled.

Then he disconnected. Reg looked at her phone for a minute, then sipped some more coffee, still piping hot.

What was eating Corvin?

CHAPTER THREE

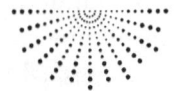

*R*eg was late.

She didn't actually *try* to be late. It *wasn't* because Corvin had grouched at her and told her not to be late, like he was a parent or a boss. He wasn't anyone in her life, and she wouldn't let even her friends talk to her that way. It was disrespectful.

It just so happened that everything was working against Reg. It took her longer to do everything, from drinking her morning coffee to showering and dressing. She nearly forgot to look at her appointments for the day, and she definitely needed to do that before going somewhere else with Corvin. If she had any afternoon appointments, she needed to know when they began so she could get back from the restaurant in time.

She hadn't realized how low the gas tank was. She'd been running on fumes when she had pulled in the previous day, but she really hadn't wanted to stop at the gas station, especially when she had Starlight in the car. She would have to leave him inside the vehicle, which she didn't like to do. Of course, you were never supposed to leave a child or animal unattended in a car. But she couldn't exactly take him out to pump the gas. And they had both been tired and irritable. Reg had been sure she could make it home. She could fill up the next day.

9

And now it was the next day and she had been rushing from one thing to another and did not want to stop for gas on her way to The Crystal Bowl. Of course, The Crystal Bowl was close enough for her to walk, but that would just make Reg tireder, angrier, and later.

So she was already flustered when she got there. She tried to force herself to slow down and relax. She took a few deep breaths to calm herself, but her heart continued to pound just as fast as it had been. She ran her fingers through her red box braids, then gathered them all together and pushed them back over her shoulders out of her way.

Bill was at the bar and nodded to her. "Are *you* the reason he is all out of sorts?"

Reg looked in the direction Bill indicated with a slight tilt of his head. Corvin sat in one of the booths, simmering. Reg could feel his heat all the way across the room. She swallowed and nodded acknowledgment to Bill.

"Yeah, I guess that's me," she admitted. "Give me a couple of cold bottles."

He obligingly grabbed a couple of beers from the fridge for her. Reg crossed the room to where Corvin sat.

Corvin didn't stand up gallantly to greet her, as he often did, but stayed slumped in his seat, dark and morose, looking at her.

"Even when I say something, you can't be here at the time we agreed?"

Reg handed him one of the cold bottles. "Here. Chill. Things just happened. I was trying to get here earlier."

Corvin didn't take the beer, scowling at it. Reg put it down on the table in front of him anyway and sat down. It wasn't like she needed him to pull out her chair for her.

Reg opened her bottle and took a long drag. She had to be careful. Getting drunk around Corvin was like shooting herself in the foot. Twice. But one beer over the course of the dinner would be fine. She would still be able to drive. And it would help her to relax and tolerate his mood better.

Corvin watched her drink, then turned his eyes to his own

bottle.

"What?" Reg asked, holding her hands palms up. "Is this brand not good enough for you, or what? I know you probably prefer whiskey, but I wanted something that was already cold and ready to drink. If you don't want it, just leave it and I'll drink it later."

"I don't take gifts of drinks. Or food of any kind."

This startled Reg at first, but she slowly processed it. "Because you were poisoned."

Corvin nodded. "I don't have any desire to go through that again."

"No. I understand why." She shrugged. "It's still sealed. If you think that someone might have tampered with it and recapped it, then don't drink it." She took another swallow of hers. "Nothing wrong with mine."

"You wouldn't have been poisoned by my drink either. It was targeted. It wouldn't have hurt you."

Because it had just been water, Reg remembered. Holy water. Nearly fatal to Corvin, but not harmful to anyone else. Only to his kind, apparently.

Reg put her bottle down on the table. "So... what did you want? It sounded pretty urgent, so..."

Normally, he would protest. He would tell her that they would save the business for after lunch, that there was no need to rush into anything, that they should make the meal as pleasant as possible. And he would exude pheromones.

This time was different. No flirty behavior. No heady smell of roses as he tried to charm her. The warm wave she felt rolling off of him was not the usual romantic flush, but the heat of his anger.

At her? It seemed silly to be that angry at her for being late when, as he had said, she was almost always late and he could have expected it, whether he told her to be on time or not. He couldn't be mad at her for something she did all the time. It was her nature. Maybe humans with her particular mix of siren and immortal blood were always late. Maybe they all had the challenges that she did with getting everything done in the proper sequence and timing so that she could be on time.

Maybe that was just what sirens were like.

Corvin leaned in closer to the table and to Reg.

"People are dying," he said in a tight, restrained whisper. He lifted his head like a gopher to look around and ensure no one was listening to them. "This isn't something to be casual or joke about."

"Okay…" Reg shook her head, impressed by his vehemence. Whatever Corvin's reason for calling her was, it was not just to tease and flirt with her. It wasn't just to have lunch with a friend because they hadn't seen each other lately. Or because they were enemies and he wanted to keep an eye on her. He was really concerned about something. "Who, exactly, is dying?"

A waitress floated over to them, order pad in hand, looking distant or dazed. "Do you want drinks?"

Corvin glared at her. Not the way he usually treated the staff that served him. "We already have drinks," he snapped, pointing to the two bottles of beer.

"Oh. What about your lunch order, then?" She looked around for menus, but Reg and Corvin had been there enough times that they didn't need them. They already knew everything backward and forward. "Have you decided?"

Corvin was impatient with the interruption. But he couldn't very well tell her to go and get what he wanted without telling her just what that was.

"Burger and fries for me," Reg said quickly, though fries were a bad idea and she should get salad along with her burger. Or instead of. She meant to put herself on a diet, as her waist was expanding a bit more than she cared to admit. But she was stressed by Corvin's behavior. And a salad wouldn't do as comfort food. "And…" she looked at Corvin, "catch of the day?" she guessed for him.

Corvin gave a curt nod.

The waitress nodded, wrote a few notes in her order pad, and retreated.

Corvin gave a huff of irritation and looked back at Reg. "Where were we?"

"People are dying?"

CHAPTER FOUR

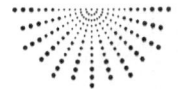

Corvin nodded.

Reg studied him. Corvin was sometimes given to drama and liked to shock. But she wasn't sure that was the case this time. His expression was drawn. There were shadows under his eyes like he hadn't slept the night before. His whole demeanor was off; everything that made him Corvin was gone. Or buried until he could sort things out.

He was still handsome, the short beard neatly trimmed, his dark eyes glittering. Looking like someone who had just stepped out of a magazine. But he was not himself. Something was definitely off.

"Who is dying?" she asked seriously, trying to mirror his expression. People unconsciously responded more positively when they were mirrored, a trick Reg had learned early in her career. It had to be very subtle—she couldn't just mimic everything—but she had honed her skills over the years and she was pretty good. A psychic had to be someone that people could trust and talk to. Clients had to feel like she was trustworthy, even though they didn't know why.

Relief flitted quickly across Corvin's face. He had been worried that she wouldn't believe him, wouldn't take him seriously. And after all of the bumps the two of them had been through, why would she?

Because she could see that he was really concerned. And if a warlock as powerful as Corvin was concerned, then pretty much everyone else should be too.

"They have been three deaths that I know of. There may be more. And if we don't stop whatever is happening... who knows how many could be killed?"

Reg swallowed. "Who died?"

"There have been three magical practitioners that I am aware of who have died in the last week. Their deaths were sudden and unexplained. Those are just people I know. I've been checking the obituaries to try to see if anyone else fits the pattern, but sometimes it takes a few days before obituaries are published. There may have been others."

"What did the police say? Didn't they do autopsies?"

"They are looking into it, but there is no sign of violence or anything suspicious, so they are just routine death investigations. I don't even know if they'll do full autopsies. And some of the tests that they do, like tox screens or testing to see if this is a rogue virus or something contagious, can take weeks or even months to come back." He leaned forward, his eyes drilling into Reg. "Three people have died in a week. How many more will die before those tests come back? And what if it picks up speed as more people are exposed? What if it becomes an epidemic before they can even identify that something is going on?"

There was a knot in Reg's stomach.

Corvin had come to her like this once before, and then it had been the draugrs. She didn't want to have to face anything like that again. She tried to focus on what Corvin was telling her.

"You don't think it's something like... the draugrs, do you?"

"Draugar?" he corrected. "No, I don't think it's anything like that. We could feel the draugar when the Witch Doctor raised them. You remember that. You remember how it felt, how strong that feeling of dread was."

Reg nodded wordlessly.

"You don't feel that now, do you?"

Reg shook her head, though she put her hand over her stomach, trying to decide exactly what she did feel. Of course she was anxious now. But what had she been feeling before she and Corvin met? She hadn't woken with that feeling of despair, like she had with the draugar. She had wondered what Corvin was going on about, but she hadn't felt them coming. Hadn't felt some horrible danger closing in on them all. When the Witch Doctor had been operating in Black Sands, she had known it. He had been too powerful to hide from her.

"No, not like that," she agreed. "Nervous about what you're saying. Worried. But not... I don't feel anything like that. Anything so... dark."

He nodded, but didn't look particularly reassured by this. "That doesn't mean nothing is happening, though," he told her. "Just that... it isn't the same kind of magic. There *is* still something out there. Someone who is targeting practitioners."

"Okay." Reg swallowed hard. It wouldn't be the first time. Just recently, she'd had to go toe-to-toe with the new leader of an ancient cabal trying to kidnap and torture magical practitioners for their powers. Now it was happening all over again? "So, who do you think it is and why do you think they're targeting practitioners?"

"I don't know. I haven't been able to find any commonalities between them. They come from different backgrounds, travel in different circles."

"And it just looks like... what? You said that it wasn't violent. There wasn't anything to make them think that it was foul play, so what was it?"

"It looks like... they just died. In their sleep, walking around, going to work. They just fell asleep and never woke up. Just like that."

Reg shook her head. Could the cabal have actually attacked more people than they had realized? They might have poppets made for all of them that had been stored somewhere else. They had assumed that they knew all of the victims and had all of the effigies that had been made, but what if they were wrong? They hadn't been able to identify everyone in the cabal. Only Chevy, the leader. And he had claimed that there were others, that they would not be able to identify everyone working with him. They were hiding in plain sight.

"Do you think… it is the cabal? Or something like it?"

"I have no idea," Corvin admitted. "And investigating it as a private citizen is proving to be… much more challenging than I had anticipated."

Reg cocked her head, looking at him. He was more than capable, a powerful warlock, the leader of one of the most ancient warlock covens in the country, a scholar and professor with several hundred years' worth of experience over her. It should have been a cinch for him.

"People don't trust me," Corvin said baldly. "I can't get in to see them. Can't get past the front door or the first question. They assume that I am there to steal their powers, and that is the end of the conversation."

Well, that was the trouble with being a power drinker. People assumed he wanted to consume their powers. Reg suppressed a smirk at this. She was glad that people knew what Corvin was and that they didn't trust him. He might be finding it frustrating, but it reassured her. She had been fighting the traditions of the magical community since she had arrived. The community considered it taboo to talk about warlocks with Corvin's affliction, which meant that the unsuspecting new members of their community had no idea what he was and were in danger if they interacted with him.

But she understood Corvin's frustration at being unable to talk to anyone about the danger he saw in the community. This time he was trying to be the protector rather than the predator, and was stymied by his nature. Or by people's knowledge of it. Something Reg had experienced herself many times.

"Who are you talking to? What are you trying to find out?"

The waitress arrived with their meals, and Reg had to wait patiently while she arranged everything and made sure they had everything they wanted before finally leaving them alone again.

"Did you go to the police?" Reg asked. "I mean, if people have been killed… that's what they do, isn't it?"

"Of course I tried that. In the past, I would have at least had the ear of one detective who might be able to tell me something. But without Marta…"

Detective Marta Jessup had vowed never to have anything to do with Corvin again, and Reg couldn't blame her for that. What Corvin had done to her and her family was unforgivable.

"I could ask her," Reg offered.

"She'll want to know where you got it from."

And if Reg said that it had come from Corvin, Marta might refuse to answer or have anything to do with the investigation into the killings.

"So I'll tell her… that I got home from my vacation and looked at the papers, and saw these three deaths, and figured…"

Corvin shook his head, scowling. "You saw it in the papers, Reg?"

"Well, didn't you say it was in the papers? That you were looking at the obituaries?"

"Sure. But Marta knows you better than that. You don't read newspapers."

"Well then I read it online. They publish them on the web too."

"And you read them."

"Well…" Reg let a few seconds of silence pass as she tried to think of what to say to that. "No."

"Of course you don't." Corvin shook his head. "You're not a reader. You're not interested in obituaries. You're not old enough to care about obituaries."

All that was true, but Reg didn't feel he was being fair to her. She *could* have cared about obituaries. She *could* have read them online. If she had wanted to. But she didn't, and she hadn't.

"Then… I heard gossip about it here." Reg made a gesture to indicate The Crystal Bowl. "People were talking about it. And I overheard. And I wanted to know what she thought."

"Nobody else is concerned about it."

"How could they not be concerned that three magical practitioners died suddenly, without warning or explanation?"

Corvin shook his head. "I wish I had an answer for you."

"People have to care."

"They don't."

"Well, maybe…" Reg tried to think of a good explanation of why they would not care about the unexplained deaths. "Maybe they figure that… they lived good, long, lives, and it wasn't anything to be concerned about."

"That's one of the weird things, though," Corvin said. "You know that practitioners live longer lives. It should be *more* startling that we've had three of our community members die suddenly within a week of each other. People *should* be concerned and asking questions, but they are not."

CHAPTER FIVE

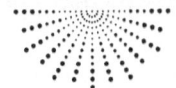

*R*eg's head was spinning as she returned home. She wasn't sure what to make of Corvin's claims. He had tempted her into things in the past, telling stories designed to garner her sympathy. He wasn't above telling her half-truths or even outright lies to manipulate her into doing what he wanted her to. She had to be careful not to take everything he said at face value. She would need to do her own investigating, and confirm that what he had said was true.

But that didn't stop her from worrying about it. If what Corvin said was true, there was no time to waste. People could die before they could figure out what was going on and who was behind the mysterious deaths. There was no time to lose.

The hamburger sat like a lead ball in her uneasy stomach. She regretted having discussed the situation over a meal. It would have been better to just meet Corvin for coffee or a walk in the park. Maybe then she wouldn't be feeling so queasy. The meal felt like it would take days to digest.

"Knock, knock!" Sarah called out as she opened the door and let herself into the cottage. "I saw you come in. How are you doing? Are you glad to be home?"

Reg was but, for an instant, she wasn't sure why Sarah was

asking and thought she might know something about her meeting with Corvin. But of course, Sarah was asking her if she was glad to be home from her vacation, not her lunch with Corvin.

"Oh, yes. It's always nice to come home. And this has really become home to me." Reg smiled and looked at the decor around her fondly. "I can't believe how long I've been here. Normally I'm in and out of a community in a few weeks or months."

Sarah laughed. "And I would consider a decade a very short stay."

"You sound like the Sas—the forest people. Etienne says he's just getting used to his house in the Everglades, and it's been something like seventy years." Reg shook her head at the thought of living anywhere for that length of time.

"Ah, when you're older, you'll understand. You're just a spring chicken. Not even a full-grown chicken, just a chick."

Reg pressed the button on the coffee maker to brew herself a cup. Maybe she'd feel better once she had enough caffeine in her.

"How were Etienne and his beloved?" Sarah asked.

"They're good... Ilka had a problem, but I got that all straightened out. It's hard to tell if their relationship will last... they are very different from humans. *Homo sapiens,*" Reg corrected herself. Etienne and his people did consider themselves human, just a different species. "Ilka seems very domineering, but he has said before that the women in his culture are very 'formidable,' so I think it's something he likes."

"They don't have divorce," Sarah reminded her. "So it will last for however long they live. There is no question of them not staying together."

"Even if she is emotionally abusive?"

"As you said, their culture is different from ours, and they prize strong personalities, so they would not see moodiness or dictatorial behavior as abuse."

"Huh." Reg had a sip of her freshly brewed cup of coffee. She motioned to the shiny new machine. "Help yourself if you want any. It's really good."

Sarah eyed the monstrosity. "I don't know what was wrong

with the old coffee maker. It worked just fine. I hope you didn't throw it out. These new-fangled machines are…" She shook her head, looking for a word, "intimidating."

Intimidating was a good word to describe Ilka too.

"It's not hard," Reg assured her. "All you have to do is put your mug underneath and press the green button." She pointed to it.

"But what about all of the other settings?"

A myriad of buttons and switches glowed on the machine's control panel. There was an app that could control it through Wi-Fi, but Reg hadn't installed it yet.

"I don't want you to change the other settings anyway. If you just want a cup of coffee, press the green button. If you want something fancier sometime when we do a girls' night, I'll set it up to make a latte or espresso."

"Oh, that would be nice," Sarah admitted. "But not an espresso before bed."

"You don't go to sleep until the early morning anyway, like me."

Sarah nodded once in agreement. "But if I have any caffeine after nine, I won't get to sleep at all."

"Then maybe we'll do a girls' morning. Afternoon," Reg amended. She wouldn't be in any mood for friendly banter early in the morning. "And we'll make fancy coffees for everyone."

"That sounds like a wonderful plan," Sarah said vaguely, her eyes drifting off to something in the middle distance that only she could see. Maybe memories of past friends and get-togethers.

After a minute, Sarah looked down at the bag she held.

"I didn't just come over here to gossip. I brought you something."

She put the paper bag on the kitchen counter. Reg leaned closer to examine the words on the label.

"Mystical Morsels?" Reg could see dark balls through the little plastic window. "Chocolate truffles?"

"Yes. You really must try them. They are so delicious. To die for."

"Well… I'll have to have one later. I've just finished my lunch, and my stomach won't be ready for anything else for a while."

"Just have one," Sarah suggested. "You'll see how good they are."

"No, not right now," Reg shook her head. She wasn't even sure she could finish the cup of coffee; her stomach was so rumbly and uncertain. She'd never been a big fan of truffles. They were so rich and always left her feeling a little queasy. Not a feeling she wanted to add to her already rocky situation. "They look lovely. I'll try one later."

Sarah looked disappointed. She shook her head. "You don't know what you are missing."

"Why don't you have one now?" Reg offered.

"Oh, no. I brought them over for you. I've already had more than are good for me."

"One more won't hurt," Reg tempted.

Sarah broke down and helped herself to one, as Reg knew she would. Sarah rolled the top of the bag down again and fastened it in place. She popped the little ball of chocolate into her mouth and then moaned in pleasure.

"You don't know what you are missing."

Reg smiled. "Thank you. I'll have one later."

"Make sure you do! I added a couple of appointments to your calendar." Sarah cupped both hands over her eyes, as though she were tired. She removed them and tapped the appointment book on the island. "Don't forget to look at your schedule. I didn't set too much up for the first few days because I figured you would want to ease back into it."

"That's perfect. Thanks."

Reg knew that instead of easing back into the psychic business, she would be jumping into the investigation of the recent deaths with both feet.

CHAPTER SIX

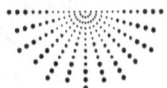

$\mathcal{D}$etective Marta Jessup was on duty and couldn't talk to Reg until later. That might have been different if Reg had wanted to make an official report. She might have been able to come much sooner. But Reg didn't want to make any kind of official report with the police. What would she say if she did? They already knew about the deaths. She couldn't exactly go to them and tell them to look at it more carefully because her warlock friend had said that it was suspicious, or that she, as a psychic, had received some kind of vision that they needed to look into it further.

So she had to wait until the end of Marta's shift and hope that choosing to wait did not put more people in danger.

Rather than trying to bring up the conversation while the TV was on and distracting them both as they munched through a takeout pizza, Reg suggested a turn around the garden. The fresh air and sunshine would be good for her and, probably, for Marta too. It would make it easier to talk about what was going on in the community casually, and yet without the distraction of electronic entertainment.

"So, how was your trip?" Marta asked. She still sounded a little stressed from work. Reg had been hoping to talk to her when she was nice and relaxed and more open to Reg's suggestions.

"It was pretty good. If you like rustic... there's no WIFI or cell signal. If you're one of those people who likes to get away from everything, then you would love Etienne's cottage. But for me, it's a little awkward. I never was much of a camper—though I liked lighting fires."

Marta laughed. "I'll just bet you did."

"Anyway. It's comfortable, good food, interesting conversation. Though there are some... cultural differences that make it a little difficult sometimes."

"Bigfoots are not known for their conversational skills."

Reg shrugged uncomfortably. "I think everyone is different. Etienne is pretty shy and is careful of what he says. But Ilka is Russian and has a different personality than Etienne. She's very... what's a polite word for not tactful?"

"Direct?"

"Yeah. Very direct. She doesn't mince words. So if she's upset about something, you know it, and if you want to find out what she thinks about you, that's not a problem at all, because she's happy to tell you. But growing up like I did, being told to keep quiet and not being allowed to say that you don't like someone or that they make you uncomfortable... it's kind of shocking."

Marta giggled at the thought. "I can imagine. Like when you're dealing with someone who blurts. You never know what's going to come out of her mouth."

"No, but you know it is going to be... direct."

They both chuckled at that.

They had been walking aimlessly around the garden, but Reg pointed to the bench by the bubbling pond and miniature waterfall, and they both sat down. Reg stared at the rippling water, wondering whether everyone else found it as soothing as she did or if that was a part of her heritage.

Marta sighed, and her shoulders lowered a little. She was, Reg hoped, relaxing and letting all of the weight of the day go.

"So, I heard through the grapevine that there were... a few deaths in the past week," she said tentatively.

"You heard through the grapevine?" Marta challenged.

"Let's say... a confidential source."

"Oh, now you have sources, do you?" Marta sipped her cocktail. "I thought that only the police had confidential sources. I thought yours were more the... ghostly sort."

"I *could* tell you that I had been contacted by Beverley Bartley's ghost."

"Why didn't you lead with that, then? I think that's a much better story."

Reg glanced sideways at Marta, trying to figure out whether she was irritated or just joking around. Did she really prefer that Reg said she had a ghostly source rather than a living person? Or was it all just in fun?

"Okay," she said slowly. "Let's say I was contacted by Beverley Bartley's ghost, then. Last night. And she said... that it wasn't an accident."

"What wasn't an accident?"

"How she died. It wasn't accidental death. Or natural causes. Someone actually killed her."

"Really, Reg." Marta shook her head. "Sometimes people just die, and you can't figure out why. Even with our advancements in medicine and technology, sometimes people just die."

"But she didn't. It doesn't make sense that so many magical practitioners died so close together."

"It's not unusual at all. We always have clusters of death. Sometimes you can explain it, and sometimes you can't. It isn't necessarily just one thing that killed them. We like to see patterns and clusters, but they don't always mean that there is a pattern. That's just the way our brains work. The way they like to classify things."

"You've had three practitioners die within a week of each other before?"

"I don't know. Probably. Beverley was old, Reg. Hundreds of years. Even though practitioners can look very young, they might be old. You can't tell just by what someone looks like."

"I know. But that doesn't explain why they all died when they did."

"Nothing explains why they died when they did. They are unexpected but natural deaths."

"Beverley died of old age?"

Marta shrugged and sipped her drink. "Old age," she agreed.

"But if magical practitioners can live for so long, then why now?"

"We can't explain it. Sometimes people terminate the spells that are keeping them young and let themselves age naturally. Or let it gradually catch up to them. Sometimes their powers just start to fail over time. It's natural for everything to come to an end, eventually. That's all that happened. Even the most powerful practitioners are still mortal. They will all still die sooner or later."

Reg thought about Sarah. She had worried more than once about what would happen when Sarah died. They'd had one close call already, and her powers had started to wane lately—at least in comparison with Corvin's powers. Sarah might have been just as strong as she ever had been, but Corvin was strong enough to counter her spells.

Reg didn't want to think about that. Either about Sarah's powers fading or Corvin's getting stronger. She couldn't do anything about either one.

"Those practitioners will be given the same examination as anyone else. If something was done to them—or just one of them —it will show up in the autopsy."

"What if it doesn't? If it's magic, it won't show up in the autopsy, will it?" Reg was pretty sure that wasn't the way autopsies worked.

"What makes you think that it was magic?"

"Because… they were all practitioners. Like you said when you were investigating the harbor attacks, magical practitioners are a minority in Black Sands, even if there are more here than anywhere else in the country. So if they all were attacked using some kind of magical spell…"

"They weren't attacked."

"You know what I mean. It doesn't even have to be direct. It could be using a Voodoo doll, like the cabal."

"A poppet," Marta corrected.

"Yes. You know what I mean."

"I just think we should be clear," Marta muttered. "Rather than assign it to one particular religion or rite."

"Yeah. Okay. I'm not saying that there are a bunch of voodoo practitioners running around killing people. I'm just saying, if it was some kind of magic like that, then you wouldn't know it, would you? It wouldn't show up in an autopsy."

"No. But other than your... insight, I haven't had any concerns expressed by anyone else in the community that there is anything to be concerned about with any of those deaths. The families are not concerned or making accusations, so why are you?"

"Maybe they don't have any family or friends. Or any family or friends who know about the other deaths. When you have a spate of deaths like this, I would just think you would look into it."

"I'll keep an eye on the files, but that's all I can offer. I haven't even been assigned to those cases. They are not considered suspicious, so I'm not likely to be. I can't just go to my boss and tell him I think we're dealing with something supernatural, because my friend had a ghostly visitor."

"You could tell him it was a confidential informant."

"But I'm not going to. Even if it was true, we have strict protocols about CIs and how they are handled and identified. They're not quite as confidential as you might think. I have to make certain disclosures. I can't just make someone up from thin air."

Reg opened her mouth to tell Marta that she was actually a real person and Marta didn't have to make anyone up, but Marta was sharp and beat Reg to the punch. "And my boss already knows who you are, so saying it came from you is not likely to get me anywhere."

Reg grimaced. She had previously talked to Marta's boss and had a pretty good idea of how he would react to Reg sticking her nose into things.

"So... I'm just supposed to stand by and let other people die."

"What other people?"

"Whoever is killing magical practitioners is not going to just stop there… they're going to keep killing."

"Who is? And why?"

"I don't know. I was hoping that you would investigate and find out!"

Marta eyed her and didn't say anything. Reg had spoken too sharply, had said too much. And it wasn't going to get her anywhere. Rather than driving Marta to look into the three killings, the accusation would just make Marta dig in her heels. She wasn't going to be any help to Reg.

Reg took a deep breath. "Corvin says that—"

CHAPTER SEVEN

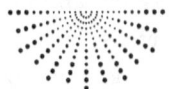

*T*his is coming from Corvin?" Marta interrupted.

Reg gritted her teeth, furious with herself for letting Corvin's name slip.

She knew better.

She *knew* that Marta wouldn't touch anything that had Corvin's name on it with a ten-foot pole.

"No, I meant that he said once—"

"You're trying to bring me in on some project initiated by Corvin? I can't believe you would do that, Reg."

"No, it's not that. I'm sure he would want you to look into it, but that isn't what I meant. I just meant that a practitioner like Corvin, he has a lot of experience and education, and so if he says something—"

"Then it's just as likely to be false as true. Come on, Reg, you know that. I'm not getting involved in a wild goose chase started by Corvin."

"I know you hate him, but won't you just consider—"

"I don't hate him," Marta said, waving this aside. "But I don't see him as the great expert on every subject, either. He might fool you with that act, but I've got his number. I just don't believe him."

"You've gone to him as an expert before."

"Yeah, I have. Sometimes to my benefit and sometimes not. I don't enjoy being called out onto the carpet when he says something that is just not true. Or is speculation. The guy has an ego as big as all outdoors, Reg. He wants people to worship him and fawn around him and, if they don't, he wants to know why not. Or to find something that will make them change their minds."

Reg had seen women of all kinds fawn over Corvin. He didn't have to do much to completely entrance those around him. In a few seconds, he could ensorcel someone to do whatever he pleased. But what he wanted wasn't just adoration. It was power. He had little interest in those fawning women if they didn't have something to give him.

Was he just trying to get Reg involved in a fake investigation so that he would have an excuse to be near her? In case the right circumstances presented themselves and he would have another chance to steal her powers?

But even though it made sense, Reg didn't think that was the case. Corvin wasn't just trying to get admiration. He wasn't just trying to steal Reg's powers. He hadn't done anything while at the restaurant to try to entice or entrance her. No pheromones, no flirting, no coaxing her to go somewhere more private with him. He had been too concerned about the deaths of his friends. The shadows under his eyes showed that it wasn't fake concern. It wasn't a made-up threat to the population of Black Sands. He wasn't sleeping. He had little interest in food, not even ordering for himself at the restaurant. When he had received the catch of the day at The Crystal Bowl, he mainly pushed it around his plate, uninterested. That wasn't the way he normally behaved.

"I really think this is something we need to be worried about," Reg told Marta earnestly. "I don't think it's just a coincidence, or Corvin grandstanding. I really think that something is going on that the police need to look into."

"I told you that I would keep an eye on the investigations. That's really all I can do. I can't control what they find during the autopsy. I can't go to my boss and say that there is a pattern when there isn't. Or that I have a reliable source that says something is going on, because…" she shrugged, looking embarrassed. "I don't trust the source. Corvin, Reg, not you. You don't know anything other than what he has told you. You're just going on what he had to say. If you knew something independently… if there was something else you could add to the story… some evidence… but you don't. And I don't have anything to go to my superiors with."

CHAPTER EIGHT

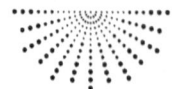

*R*eg returned to the cottage, angry and frustrated. She had known that going to Marta was a long shot. She had known what answer she was going to get before she asked. But she still had to ask.

Now what was her next step?

Starlight wound around Reg's ankles, yowling urgently. If she didn't know what she was supposed to do next, she was stupid. It was time for the human to feed the feline. Everything in its proper order.

"Careful... watch out..." Reg muttered as she moved around the island, trying not to trip or kick Starlight with each step. Starlight could see she was moving toward the fridge. Why didn't he just let her walk the rest of the way unimpeded?

Who could question the nature of a cat?

"I'm getting it for you," Reg told Starlight as he started to yowl again when she pulled a bowl of tuna out of the fridge. "This isn't just my dinner. You'll get yours."

Eventually, she had Starlight settled down, eating his dinner. Which still left Reg's to be prepared. But she wasn't hungry yet. She should wait until she was hungry.

She looked at the bag of truffles that was still on the counter. Sarah had been kind to bring them by. She often brought Reg food, though usually, she was trying to get Reg to eat better. Truffles were a bit of a departure from the home-cooked meat and vegetable fare Sarah normally brought. She had probably been given them by someone else and found that there were too many for her to eat on her own. Maybe, like Reg, she found them too rich.

Reg grabbed the bag and unclipped the wire ties that held the rolled-up top of the bag closed. She unrolled it and stuck her nose into the top. They did smell very good. Reg was reminded of the warm brownie scent that Corvin's son, John, exuded. She had to admit she was tempted by them despite her past experiences with truffles.

Starlight looked up from his dish and gave a mournful-sounding howl. Reg frowned, studying him.

"Are you okay, Star? Are you going to throw up?"

It was similar to the howl that he would make before upchucking a meal consumed too quickly. But not quite the same. She couldn't be sure if that was what he was telling her.

Starlight stared at her for a minute, then returned to eating. Apparently, his stomach wasn't hurting too badly.

Reg checked her appointment calendar and decided she'd better start preparing for her evening readings.

* * *

Early in the morning, Reg was failing at falling asleep. It had been a long and busy day. She had taken care of all the pre-sleep routines that she normally did, and even had a cup of sleepy tea to help calm her brain and body down. But it wasn't working. Her brain was still going a mile a minute and she couldn't set her worries aside.

She tossed and turned for way too long. She wandered around the cottage and went back to bed. She turned down the AC. She hummed to herself, rocked back and forth, and even tried a lullaby.

Which probably would have gone better if she had known more than the first line or two.

Reg rubbed her face, trying to relax all of the muscles. If everything was relaxed, she would fall asleep.

She looked at her phone again to see what time it was, sure she was going to see it was almost time for the normal people to get up. The day shift people. The joggers and office workers and other people who intentionally got out of bed ridiculously early. But it was still too early even for them.

The phone rang in her hand and, of course, Reg knew who it was before the name came up on the screen.

"Why are you still up?" she asked Corvin.

He laughed mirthlessly. "Why are you?"

"I'm trying to remedy that. Which isn't helped by the fact that you're interrupting me."

"Did you talk to Marta? Have you made any decision on how to proceed?"

"I talked to her, but... it's like we both figured. She won't do anything about it. They all think it is perfectly normal. Just a coincidence. Nothing to indicate that it is anything other than natural causes."

"What happened? Did their hearts just stop?"

"I don't know. Autopsy results are not in yet. We'll have to wait and see if anything shows up in the reports."

Corvin swore under his breath.

Reg sighed. "Sorry, did what I could. Did you... know these people personally? Is that why you noticed a pattern?"

"I knew them or their families. The magical community in Black Sands is a good size but, if you've been in town for as long as I have... you have acquaintances in all of the old families. You can understand why I can't just look the other way."

"I can," Reg agreed. "But I don't know how I can help. I don't have any evidence of anything and neither do you. It's just speculation based on... math. An unusual number of people dying in one week."

"Yeah. Do you *want* to help?"

"Yes, I would if I could. But I don't think there is anything I can do."

"Would you go out with me tomorrow—or later today, I guess —and talk to the families?"

"The families of the people who died?"

"Yes. Exactly. How else are we going to figure out what happened?"

"I don't know. I don't know how talking to the families is going to help, really."

"It's more likely to be productive than sitting around grousing that we don't know anything."

"Well, yeah. I guess so. I guess if you're going to do the visits, I could come along. As long as you're in charge, I don't know these people or what to ask them."

"Yes, I'll do the introductions," Corvin agreed grouchily. "I'm not just pushing you into this on your own. And as far as your value in such an... experiment... you're a woman. You're psychic. You're easy to talk to. You're far more likely to get something out of them than I am. People just clam up when I ask them questions."

"I doubt it. I've seen the way other people are around you. They're falling all over themselves to do what you want. If you ask questions, they'll tell you their life stories."

"Most of the people you are referring to are nonmagical," Corvin pointed out. "Waitresses and hostesses. People who are only nominally connected to the magical community. I don't want their life stories or anything else from them. But the people who know me and what I am... They are not likely to fall all over themselves to answer me. They will be... hesitant if not downright confrontational."

"Even though you were friends?"

"I didn't say we were friends. I said that I knew them or their families. Ancient families from this area are not likely to be friends with a warlock bearing the name Hunter."

Reg felt bad for Corvin for being an outcast from his own community and, at the same time, glad that families in the community were still holding strong against him. She worried about the women who crossed Corvin's path without knowing what he was. With it being taboo to even talk about Corvin's hunger and his need to feed on others' powers, she worried that others like her would surrender their powers to him when she had only intended to consent to an intimate evening.

"Were all of the men in your Hunter line… like you?"

"No. Not all of them. But that didn't matter. They were still pariahs just because of the family name, whether they bore the curse or not. It was even worse for them. Being hated for their family, when they didn't even have the power to do the thing that everyone feared. If you're going to be hated… you may as well *be* the thing you are hated for."

Reg made a noise of understanding.

"So you'll go with me tomorrow?" Corvin asked.

"Yeah, I guess. If you're the only one who thinks that there is really something going on… then I guess it's up to you to try to get some evidence. I don't know anything. I'm just following your lead."

"You only think there is something there because I said so?" Corvin demanded.

"Well… yeah. I don't think that you're making things up or overreacting. I've seen enough weird stuff in Black Sands not to expect everything to make sense. If something bad is happening, then something bad is happening. If you say it isn't normal and you think there might be a threat to the rest of the community… then I'll help you out. If it ends up being nothing, then it's nothing."

"It isn't," he assured her.

Reg nodded. "I don't think it is."

CHAPTER NINE

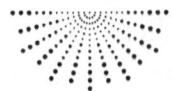

*R*eg had gotten to sleep too late to have Corvin picking her up so early in the morning. The birds were still chirping in the trees, for goodness' sake. And chirping way too loudly for Reg's liking.

She held her large flask of coffee in her lap. She wasn't going anywhere without coffee, and lots of it. She rubbed her forehead as Corvin drove them to their first destination, Beverley Bartley's family. Reg had no idea how that would go or how they would be received. Would the family be happy to see Corvin because he was trying to help? Afraid of him because of his nature? Would they think that he had done something that had contributed to Beverley's death?

"You don't need to be so worried," Corvin told her. But his hands on the steering wheel were white-knuckled. She knew him well enough to know that wasn't normal. He was not usually a stressed driver.

"I just don't know what they'll think of us showing up and asking questions."

"They'll be happy about it," Corvin told her. "Wouldn't you be happy if someone came to you to tell you they were sorry about the death of your loved one and wanted to help out in some way? Even if they don't think there was foul play, they'll know we're just there to help."

Reg wasn't so sure. But she tried to appear less anxious. Her mood was probably making Corvin's worse. If they were going to get answers out of Beverley's family, they needed to be relaxed and feel like they were somewhere safe. If everyone in the room were amped up and anxious, they would be too, and the discussion would go nowhere.

The house that they pulled up to wasn't anything out of the ordinary. The street looked like any other street in Black Sands and the houses on it were similar to Sarah's in age and appearance. Large for single-family homes, but she had noticed that was common in many small towns. The property didn't cost as much money, so they spent more on building the house. And maybe historically, the families that lived there had raised large families, with eight or ten kids. With families having just one or two chil-dren now, there was a lot of extra space for home offices, TV viewing rooms, and other uses.

She went with Corvin up the sidewalk, not wanting to follow him and appear shy or subservient, but also not wanting to lead the way. He was the one who knew these people and would have to introduce himself at the door, not Reg. So she walked beside and just a little behind him, as the sidewalk was too narrow to walk side by side and she couldn't exactly walk through the flower border or on the lawn beside him.

The Bartley family was apparently not watching for their approach. They did not open the door as soon as Corvin and Reg arrived at the door, as Reg had expected. Instead, they had to wait after Corvin pressed the doorbell. He glanced over at her as they waited, saying nothing. He seemed irritated at having to wait. He had expected them to be grateful for his visit.

Eventually, the door opened, and a short, slight woman with gray hair peered out at them.

"Yes...?"

"I'm Corvin Hunter, ma'am," Corvin introduced himself expectantly. "I came to see you about Beverley?"

"Oh. About Bev." The woman paused momentarily to consider this, then apparently decided to speak with them. She opened the door farther and ushered them in. The living room was dim, and their host turned on a few lights that didn't make much of a difference. She looked around as if she hadn't been there for a long time and didn't know what condition she would find it in. Surely she'd had a lot of visitors the past few days as she and her family had mourned Bev's passing.

She picked up some newspapers spread out on the couch and left them in a messy pile on the coffee table, motioning for Reg and Corvin to take a seat. Reg would have preferred to sit in one of the easy chairs, not so close to Corvin, but they were covered with various other newspapers, books, glasses, and crumby plates. The woman cleared one for herself, but Reg figured it would be rude for her to do the same when she had instructed them to take a seat on the couch.

She sat next to Corvin, keeping as far away from him as possible. She was sure he wouldn't try to ensorcel her in front of the woman, but one could never be too careful. Reg looked around after they were all seated.

"I'm sorry… I didn't get your name."

"Helen. Helen Papadakis."

There was no way Reg was going to remember that.

"Are you the only one here, then?" she asked, "you live by yourself?"

"The others are around," Helen said, making a movement with her hand that conveyed that they were in various parts of the house doing their own thing. Reg reached out her senses toward the other members of the family. It didn't feel like a house of mourning. Everyone was just occupied with their own activities and didn't seem interested in Corvin being there to ask questions about Bev.

"Will any of them be joining us?"

"No… I don't think so."

There was a somewhat awkward pause.

"I was very sorry to hear about Beverley," Corvin said eventually.

"Yes, it was something of a shock," Helen agreed.

"It was very sudden, wasn't it? She didn't have any health issues that you were aware of?"

"No, she seemed very healthy up until the last few days. Then... she was a little pale, maybe. Not as interested in her work. And then..." Helen shrugged and spread her hands apart, palms up. "And then she was gone."

"Do you think she was sick?"

"No. No, she didn't seem sick. Maybe she just sensed... that the end was approaching."

"Bev was your... daughter?" Reg asked tentatively. She should have asked Corvin about the family relationships before they arrived. But she had expected a larger group and proper introductions.

"My sister. My twin sister."

"Oh, I'm so sorry!" Reg reached out, feeling for Bev's presence in the house, attached to her sister. Twins were closely connected psychically in life. Reg wouldn't expect Bev to be far from her sister in death. She closed her eyes and stretched out further for Bev's presence.

Her mind flooded with memories. Two little blond girls running in a sunny field, cheeks flushed pink, laughing as they played tag, hitching up their skirts to run. Flopping down on their backs, exhausted, basking in the warm sun, staring up at a brilliant blue sky and fluffy white clouds. The sort of idyllic childhood Reg had never experienced. No siblings of her own, no sunny field.

But she'd had Erin, one of her foster sisters. Not playing tag in a sunny summer field, but picking bottles, hiding in back alleys so they wouldn't get caught helping themselves to other people's empties, giggling and getting into trouble.

Reg needed to call Erin. It had been too long since they had seen each other last and Reg wanted to be with her, to know she was okay, and to share a few of those memories once again.

"You and your sister loved each other," Reg told Helen. "You were inseparable. Identical. It must be very hard for you to be separated now."

"I suppose so," Helen agreed with a shrug. "I figure that since she is gone… I won't likely be too far behind. We always did things together."

Maybe that was why Reg wasn't getting the feeling she normally did from mourners. Helen wasn't mourning her sister because she expected to join her soon. Reg looked over at Corvin, wondering if this was one of the deaths Corvin hoped to help prevent. He pressed his lips together and gave a very slight incline of his head, acknowledging the look.

CHAPTER TEN

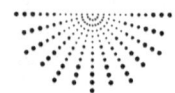

"So she was feeling poorly before she passed?" Corvin asked, trying to bring the conversation back on track. "You thought she might be sick?"

"Well, I didn't think so. I just thought... maybe she was feeling off. Blue. She got like that sometimes. I didn't think it was anything different. Maybe she was a little pale and just needed a bit of sunshine. But then it was too late. I didn't know."

"She got depressed? Was she having any other mental issues that you know of? Or... anyone that she was having trouble with?"

"Bev got along with everybody. *You* should know that."

Corvin flushed a little, red creeping up his neck from under his shirt collar. He ran his finger along the inside of his collar, giving a thin smile.

"She was always nice to me," he admitted. "Which was not true of most people. She was somebody special."

"She was," Helen agreed with a distant smile.

"She didn't have... an ex-husband or anyone from the past that wanted to get back at her for something?"

"No, of course not. She was never married. Always very popular with the boys. But she was a spinster."

While Helen had gone on to marry and raise a family in this house.

"Did she live here with you?" Reg asked.

"Yes. Always. Other than when George and I first got married. For a few months... a year... but I couldn't stand to be separated. Knowing that she was alone. So we asked her to come and live with us. Made sure she had a little suite of her own. But she always had dinner with the family. Spent the day with me. Helped with the children. Family should be together."

Reg nodded her agreement. "That was very nice of you."

Helen nodded. She looked vaguely around the room, then her eyes turned back to them as if she didn't know why they were there.

"It's just me, now. Me and my children."

"You must really miss her."

"I'm sure we'll see each other again soon."

Reg found the apathy in her tone alarming. She didn't know what to say.

Corvin spoke up again. "Bev hadn't been sick or had trouble with anyone... did anything strange happen lately? Phone hang-ups? A visit from an old acquaintance? Somebody angry at her, seemingly for no reason?"

Helen shook her head. "No, nothing like that. Everything was just normal." She shrugged. "I don't really know why you're asking. She just died in her bed. The police didn't ask any questions. They said that it had to go to the medical examiner's office, but other than that... we would be able to have the funeral in a few days to take care of her."

"It's just that... I don't know if you have heard of any of the other deaths in the past week. Patty Meiers and Andy Shoop...?"

She shook her head. Her eyes went to the window and she watched something Reg couldn't see. Maybe not outside, but memories of the past playing before her eyes.

"Did she... eat anything before bed?" Corvin tried. "Did she say how she was feeling before she went to bed? Nauseated or in any pain?"

"No, nothing... We probably ate before bed. We usually do."

Helen shrugged. "We like something sweet or salty before bed. I know they say you're not supposed to eat between supper and bedtime, but life's little pleasures…"

Corvin nodded. "What did she have?"

"That night? I'm not sure. Popcorn, I think. But she didn't die from eating popcorn."

"That's all?"

"I don't know. I don't monitor what she eats. I know we had popcorn together."

"With drinks?"

"She only drinks water."

Corvin frowned. "What about for supper? Earlier in the day?"

"You want to know everything she ate?" A W-shaped frown line appeared between Helen's brows.

"How long do you think she had been feeling poorly?" Reg inserted.

"A few days, I don't know. She was pale and kind of… irritable. I didn't know that it was anything serious. And I still don't think it was. I think… it was just her time." She sighed. "Maybe it's time for both of us."

Reg shook her head, looking at Corvin. "It couldn't be something she ate the night before, then. Not if she seemed like she was 'off' for several days."

Corvin grimaced and tried to think of some other way to approach it. "Had anything changed the last few days? Her diet? Someone new in her life? Some new habit or change in her routine?"

"No. I'm sorry, I can't think of anything. I think it was probably just a coincidence that those other people died too."

"Did Bev know the others? Were they friends or working on a project together, anything like that?"

"No, I don't think so. We knew who they were, but we didn't have anything particular to do with them."

"Did Bev have a boyfriend? Did she work?"

Helen stood up and wandered around the room, looking at the various pictures, lamps, and other decorations and touching them tentatively as if trying to remember where she had gotten them or was afraid that they would vanish away now that her twin was gone.

"She didn't have a boyfriend. Bev was never that interested in men. Or in anyone. That's just the way she was. There wasn't anything wrong with her," Helen raised her voice a little, sounding defensive.

"No, of course not. Some people just aren't that interested in a romantic relationship," Corvin assured her.

"And she hadn't worked for years. We both decided to retire and just enjoy life. The house was paid for, of course. It hardly cost anything when we built it. We had money put away, both George and I and Bev. Enough that we didn't have to worry about working. It's probably been… sixty years since we retired."

The number boggled Reg's mind. At a minimum, that would make the woman before her one hundred and twenty. Given the numbers she had heard from other magical practitioners, she was probably double that, maybe even more.

What would Reg do if she lived that long? She assumed that she would retire. She would get bored of doing readings and seances sooner or later. When she had seen and done it all, she would probably want to take a break. Or start something new.

But maybe, like Helen, she would just tire of life and decide it was her time. Corvin had talked about being alone, about how difficult it was to keep losing the people he loved. All of his non-practicing friends would die long before him. If it were Reg, then maybe she *would* be ready to just gracefully meet her end.

Maybe that was all that had happened to Beverley. She had just decided that it was time to go.

CHAPTER ELEVEN

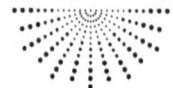

*T*here wasn't much more to be accomplished by talking with Helen, so they thanked her and excused themselves. She made no effort to keep them there. Most of the older women Reg knew would have wanted to talk about her memories of her sister and their childhood together. But Helen didn't seem to be engaged with the discussion. She was happy to let them go.

Reg shook her head as they walked back to the car. She sat down in the passenger seat and looked at Corvin.

"That's really sad. It's like she's just given up now that her sister is gone."

"I was really hoping to be able to get more out of her." Corvin drummed his fingers on the steering wheel, scowling. "They make it look so easy on TV, don't they? You just ask a few questions, and the answer drops into your lap. Maybe it takes a few days or a few interviews but, eventually, you come to realize the meaning of something they told you, and it all falls into place…"

"Well, we haven't had time to ponder or discuss it yet. And Helen was only the first interviewee. You have others?"

"But if they're all like that… I was sure she would want to know what had happened to her sister. Why wouldn't she want to know the truth? Why wasn't she demanding it?"

"Because she doesn't think there's anything to find out."

"Even when she heard about the others? Doesn't she see that this is more than just a coincidence?"

"No one else does yet."

Corvin looked at her as he pulled out into the street. "Including you?"

"I don't know yet. Maybe when we've talked to the others. Right now... I'm just going on your say-so." She shrugged one shoulder. "You're a pretty smart, experienced guy. I'll go with it until I've seen and heard enough to make up my own mind one way or the other."

"Well... I'd rather you thought the same thing as I do, but I guess I'll have to take that. You're willing to accept my opinion for the time being..."

"That's why I'm here."

He nodded. "Okay."

He drove in silence for a few minutes.

"Who is next on the list?" Reg asked.

"I'm going in order of the victims' deaths, so the next one is Patty Meiers."

"And is she the same story? An older woman, just died in her sleep?"

"I'll let you find out during the interview. I don't want to bias you. Come to your own conclusion about Patty Meiers."

Reg blinked, thinking about it. "Okay... you don't want to give me a hint?"

"Nope."

Reg looked at him, but he gave nothing away by his expression. She touched his mind, but all that she could feel was the anger and frustration that he had already expressed. Anything else was either buried deeper or he was blocking her somehow.

Patty Meiers's house was on a poorer street. Townhouses built one right up against the other. Children playing in the street turned around and glared at the approaching car as if Corvin and Reg had done something wrong.

Reg remembered the children she had seen playing when they

were looking for Calliopia the fairy. As it turned out, what she thought were children were actually pixies, lookouts for their colony.

Reg scrutinized the closest children, trying to discern whether they were actually human children or whether they were pixies or some other species. Corvin had the hint of a smile on his face, watching her covertly.

"I just want to know if they are really children," Reg snapped at him. "Or if they're something else."

"Look like children to me."

"But so do pixies."

"I think I would know if they were pixies. They would have brown, curly hair and rosy pink cheeks. These children are more..." He gazed out at them, searching for a word. "Gaunt. Human."

Reg had to admit that she couldn't see anything that would give away that they were anything more than they appeared to be. Regular human children.

Corvin drove slowly since the children did not all get off of the road ahead of him. He wove around them until he reached the townhouse number he sought.

"Will your car be safe?" Reg asked as they got out and Corvin locked the doors.

"I'm arming the alarm."

"Do you think that will stop them?"

"I'm hoping. It will at least be enough to tell us that they *aren't* leaving it alone."

Reg walked up the sidewalk with Corvin. The sidewalk up to the house was two sidewalk blocks wide, so there was enough room for Reg to stay at Corvin's side and, even if she didn't stay on the sidewalk, there were no flowers or lawn to be trampled.

This time, someone was watching for them, or had been warned by one of the little hooligans playing outside. The door opened promptly when they were halfway up the sidewalk.

The woman who answered the door was the opposite in every way to Helen. She appeared to be in her early twenties. She was tall and stood confidently, shoulders back. She had numerous piercings and tattoos. Her black hair was cut close to the scalp. So close it might have been shaven down to the skin a few days before. The woman studied Corvin and Reg, scowling.

"Who are you?"

"I called you on the phone," Corvin reminded her. "Corvin Hunter. I wanted to talk to you about your... Patty."

"What about Patty? You're not a cop."

"No, I'm not. I am just worried about what is happening in the community. Patty's death. A couple of other people that I know of. I'm worried that their deaths might be suspicious. That there is something going on, someone out there who is... who caused their deaths."

"No one killed Patty. Or she did it herself. Whichever school of thought you subscribe to."

"I know that... the police didn't see anything suspicious. But they could be wrong. It is suspicious that three people like Patty all died so close together."

"Like Patty?" the woman challenged.

Corvin looked at her, then at Reg. "Do you think we could come inside? It would be better than discussing this out in the open."

"I don't have anything to hide. Do you?"

"Well... yes. I guess I do."

The woman looked at Corvin for a moment, her expression speculative, and then nodded. "I suppose, then. But the place hasn't been cleaned, so enter at your own risk."

CHAPTER TWELVE

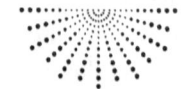

*R*eg wasn't sure what to expect inside. She'd been in some pretty nasty places before. She hoped this wouldn't rival any of them.

There were shoes and packing boxes in the front entryway. But they looked like they had been there a long time, not like she was in the middle of moving in or out. Just like they had been dumped there a couple of years ago and never unpacked and moved. She and Corvin shuffled around them. They were not asked to take off their shoes, like they had been in Egypt, and Reg was glad to be able to keep them on to avoid being contaminated by anything on the floor of the house.

She wasn't sure what color the carpet had originally been, or even if it had been one color or patterned. It was dark, worn, and so stained in different patches that there was no way to tell for sure. The woman didn't bother to have them sit down in the living room. With the amount of junk and detritus that had collected there, Reg couldn't say that she was surprised. They walked through to the kitchen. Old lino floor, sticky, holes worn and ripped here and there. A coffee maker sat on the counter, but appeared to be the only operating piece of equipment. Dirty plates covered most of the surfaces, along with takeout containers piled high on the table and in stacks on the floor, some of them empty, others with dark globs of rotting or petrifying food. Where Reg might have expected to see boxes of cereal in the open cupboard, there were boxes of cookies and sweets.

Reg didn't look for signs of cockroaches or rats. She could smell the rats as soon as she stepped into the house. The roaches were probably hiding in and under all of the food containers. It was vile. But not the worst place Reg had ever seen.

The woman leaned against the chipped Arborite counter, looking at Reg and Corvin.

"You can sit down," she said, gesturing to a couple of chairs beside the table. They looked like they had been manufactured in the seventies. And been there ever since. Neither Reg nor Corvin cleared off a chair to sit.

"Just who are you?" the woman asked Reg. "He at least told me his name. You don't have one?"

"Reg Rawlins. And you?"

The woman let out a hard laugh. "Chelsea. And it doesn't matter what my last name is. We're never going to see each other again."

"Chelsea." Reg nodded and didn't extend her hand to shake. "Nice to meet you."

Chelsea snorted. "I'll bet you're already regretting coming here."

"I didn't say that."

"You don't need to. I can see it in your face. At least this one," Chelsea nodded to Corvin, "does a better job of hiding his feelings than you do."

"Does he?" Reg looked at Corvin and shook her head slightly. "I've never had any trouble telling what he is thinking or feeling."

She might have the unfair advantage of being a psychic and sharing an unbreakable connection with Corvin. But that was beside the point.

"Would you rather I hid my feelings?" she asked Chelsea. "I always prefer knowing what people are feeling."

Chelsea considered this, then gave a slight nod. "Yeah. Maybe. Patty woulda liked you."

Reg was inordinately pleased by the comment. "What was she like?"

Chelsea sighed. "She was my best friend. She was a lot of fun. The kind of person who was there when you needed her."

"Sounds like a good best friend to have."

"She was. We didn't know each other for a long time, but we really clicked, you know? We got along and we understood each other." Chelsea twisted an earring around and around in its hole.

"Do you think that it was something other than a natural death? What you said about maybe she killed herself..."

"I don't mean suicide. I just mean... you know. Choices. Lifestyle. Neither of us leads a particularly safe life. We want to experience life to its fullest. And I guess... maybe she pushed it too far."

"Do you mean... drugs?" Reg guessed. Chelsea was thin, her arms wasted-looking. Her pupils were dilated, pools of darkness.

"She did some stuff," Chelsea admitted. "I never thought she overdid it. But she liked to party. Maybe she took a bad combination. Or it was cut with something dangerous. I don't know. Maybe she had some needle disease that she didn't know about. Or something that, you know, she got from someone else."

Chelsea pulled out a cigarette and lighter as if to demonstrate how little they had cared about how they treated their bodies. She lit it without even bothering to crack the window.

"We're not paragons of virtue. What is the point of life if you can't experience it? What is the point of cutting yourself off from half of life's experiences because of fear? Go ahead, make the decisions you want to, and see what happens. We were happier here than we ever were at any of the places we lived before we met."

Reg could understand the freedom of leaving behind the constraints of family and society to just live as she wanted. For her, that had never included drugs or any behaviors that she considered particularly dangerous, but she'd always been the person who had to test out everything her foster parents told her not to do to find out why. She wasn't the kind of person who learned from other people's mistakes, which meant she'd had the opportunity to make plenty of her own. Maybe it was surprising that she had survived through the "experimental" phase of her life.

"Did Patty live here with you?"

Chelsea blew out a stream of smoke and then made a show of waving it away from her company. That didn't stop them from getting a good blast of cigarette smoke that made Reg's nostrils flare. A band of pressure tightened around her head in response.

"Yeah. She lived here. Two friends supporting each other on their own. You think there's something wrong with that?"

Reg was bemused by the accusation. "No. I don't see anything wrong with that. It's nice. I'm glad you'll be able to show us where she lived. Her bedroom," Reg prompted, in case Chelsea wasn't following her request, "so we can get a feeling for what happened before she died?"

"I told you the cops don't think it was anything suspicious. Why should you need to see her room?"

"Is there something you're afraid to show us?" Corvin asked, intentionally annoying her with the use of the word "afraid."

Chelsea shook her head bullishly, her cheeks flushing. Her aura took on a decidedly purple shade. "No, I'm not afraid of anything. I just don't see why you need to. Her death didn't have anything to do with anyone else's. I don't know who those other people you're talking about are, but they aren't connected to Patty."

"They were both part of the same community."

"This community?" Chelsea demanded, spreading her hands apart to indicate the house and its neighbors. "I didn't know them. They didn't live anywhere near here."

"I'm talking about… her gifts," Corvin said carefully. One had to be careful about how he broached the subject of magic with others, even in a place like Black Sands where there were so many practitioners. There were still plenty of people living in the town who knew nothing about the magical community around them.

CHAPTER THIRTEEN

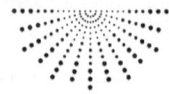

$\mathcal{C}$helsea stared at Corvin blankly for a few seconds before laughing. "You're not talking about all of that *witchy* stuff, are you?"

"Yes. I am. The other two who died were also... practicing witches. And I'm afraid there might be more to that connection... and others may still be in danger."

"I always told her that stuff was just crazy talk. I never believed a word of it, but her crazy parents raised her that way, you know? They had her convinced that she actually had magical powers. Crazy, right? But she thought she could do things with these magical gifts. She was always doing these weird rituals, and I learned just not to ask. She could do her thing, and I would do mine, and we'd enjoy each other's company when we got together for drinks or spent a night at home, or whatever. I just... let Patty be Patty, you know?"

"Patty *did* have magical gifts," Corvin affirmed. "But I guess that has nothing to do with our conversation. It doesn't matter if you believed that she was gifted or not. Just... the consequences. What happened to her."

"What were the circumstances of her death?" Reg asked tentatively, since Corvin had refused to tell her. "I'm sorry; I hope it's okay to ask that. I just know she died. I don't know how."

Chelsea gestured impatiently with her cigarette as she spoke. "It's not funny, you know. It's one of those things that people are always going to joke about or at least snicker behind their hands about. But it's not funny and no one wants to hear the jokes."

Reg nodded.

"She died, like, on the john. Downtown in the city in a club. Went to the ladies' room and never came out. I went looking for her and found her there, slumped over, sitting on the toilet." Chelsea shook her head. "I knew she was dead. I tried to find her pulse or feel her breath or something, but I knew. I called 9-1-1 and the cops came and checked things out. They said it was probably a drug overdose; that's usually what it is. But Patty didn't take a lot at a time. I guess maybe... her heart just gave out. She couldn't handle it anymore. Maybe she had a birth defect they never knew about. Or maybe, like I say, it was contaminated."

"If it was an overdose, then the medical examiner should be able to verify it pretty quickly," Reg said. "They haven't called you back yet?"

"No. They say they'll get back to me when they know something, and when I called them back about it, they said that the lab is backed up, you know the whole story. We aren't important enough to be at the front of the queue. We get in behind everybody else. Because she doesn't have any wealthy or rich relatives to push it through."

Reg had experienced plenty of prejudice against the poor in her lifetime. She knew what Chelsea meant. And even if it wasn't true, it certainly felt true. Those who had rich and powerful relatives waiting on those results got answers a lot more quickly than those who were on the street and waited for weeks for the same results, if anyone ever bothered to call them back at all.

"I have a friend who is a cop," she told Chelsea. "She probably can't do anything to get it processed faster, but I can ask her. Never hurts to ask."

"Yeah?" Chelsea shrugged as if it didn't matter. "Even if they don't find anything, they're probably going to say it's drugs. Just something that they couldn't identify. One of those new designer drugs. Or something she picked out of a ditch."

"Did she... experiment with a lot of different things?"

"Patty's drugs of choice were weed and chocolate. You really can't get much safer than that. Sure, she'd tried other stuff. Because how are you supposed to know if you like it or what it will do for you if you don't try? But she wasn't big on the hard drugs. There's more risk—not just medically, but getting caught and thrown in prison because you happened to have too much on you. Nobody really cares about weed. They're going to make it legal, you know. Anyone will be able to grow it and use it, and the cops won't be able to do anything about it. It's not like they *want* to spend their time on petty stuff like that. What cop wants to spend all their time chasing stoners who just want to get in their groove."

"And you don't think she had anything else that night?"

"No. I don't even know if she had any weed on her. Maybe some edibles. Gummies. But... she just wanted to mellow out. She wasn't a coke- or meth-head."

"Had she been feeling okay before that? She wasn't just recovering from being sick?"

Chelsea pursed her lips and shook her head. But there was something hesitant about it.

"She hadn't been sick?" Reg persisted. "Or a little bit *off?*"

"I don't know. Maybe. She was pale, kind of lethargic. I didn't think much of it. We all go through that stuff, you know. Have 'off' days. I don't think it has anything to do with her dying. How could it? She wasn't that sick, if she was sick at all. I don't see how it could have had anything to do with her dying in that bathroom."

"Her death might not have had anything to do with drugs or the location she was in," Corvin pointed out. "It might have happened at home. She could have died in her sleep, like one of the others who died two days before her."

"It wasn't a drug overdose," Chelsea said. "I know it wasn't a drug overdose, no matter what the cops say."

"I don't think it was either," Corvin agreed.

Reg could feel Chelsea's feelings toward Corvin thaw a little. She might seem tough or try to put up a tough front, but she had just lost her best friend, and people were probably judging both of them. Blaming Patty for her own death. Blaming Chelsea for it. Chelsea probably blamed herself for not stopping her friend from doing whatever it was that had killed her, especially if it really was a drug overdose. Why hadn't she seen how dangerous it was? Why hadn't she stopped Patty before it got to that point?

It was good for her to have someone who pointed away from drugs and said that there was something else at work, even if he couldn't identify exactly what that was.

"And you think it was magic?" she asked Corvin in an accusing tone, as if he had said something wrong instead of something that made her feel better. "That some wizard came and killed her while she sat on the toilet? Or she did some spell that backfired on her? Come on. You don't expect me to believe anything like that."

"I don't tell anyone what they should believe. I know that Patty had gifts. I think that if you were honest with yourself, you would recognize that she did too. You know she had special, unusual talents."

"She was just like anyone. Just like me. There isn't any such thing as magic."

"Okay." Corvin shrugged. "You don't have to believe to talk to me."

Chelsea stubbed her cigarette out impatiently in a dish on the counter. "I've answered your questions, and I can see this isn't going anywhere. I need to get ready for work. So you can show yourselves out. I don't have the time for any more of this."

Corvin opened his mouth to argue. He still wanted to see Patty's bedroom. For Chelsea to answer a few more questions on what had happened in the days before her death. But that wasn't going to happen. Chelsea had made a decision. She wasn't going to back down.

"All right," Reg agreed, cutting Corvin off before he could raise a fuss. "We'll go. But if you think of something else... if you want to talk to us about it, especially after you get the medical examiner's report back, then give us a call." Reg rummaged around in her shoulder bag until she found her business card holder and handed Chelsea one of the beautiful, colorful business cards she'd had made up. *Reg Rawlins, Psychic, Medium, Spiritual Advisor.*

Chelsea took the card and rolled her eyes when she read it.

"You might want my services someday," Reg told her. "Maybe when you would like to talk to Patty again. She's not gone, you know. Not completely. You could still talk with her again."

"I don't believe in all of that mumbo-jumbo. Sorry."

"Well, if you change your mind, you have my card. And Corvin is very knowledgeable, if you have questions about what happened to Patty." Reg looked at Corvin. He reached into his breast pocket and produced a business card of his own with a flourish. His card was black with white letters and seemed to shimmer in Chelsea's hand as she turned it over and examined it.

"Professor of what?" Chelsea asked, after turning it to the front again.

"I have multiple degrees and areas of study. I would be happy to help you in any way I can."

She gave them more attitude, rolling her eyes and shaking her head. "I don't need any help from kooks like you. It's nice that you're all concerned about Patty and these other people, but give it a rest. Nobody needs your help."

She ushered them back out to the door, even though she had told them to show themselves out. Maybe she figured she'd better make sure they left without looking at or touching anything. What looked like junk to Reg might have importance or significance to her.

CHAPTER FOURTEEN

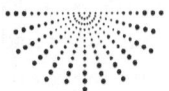

*CW*ell… that was not the result I was hoping for," Corvin grumbled as he climbed back into the car and started the engine. The car was, remarkably, untouched. It didn't look like anyone had been interested in it. Reg had expected there would at least be a few people giving it the eye, trying to decide whether it was worth stealing or just letting the air out of the tires to inconvenience the owner.

"I feel bad for her. She's so young," Reg observed.

"She doesn't even know how young she is. She thinks she's learned all there is to know about the world, but there is so much more out there," Corvin sighed. "After living so many years… I am still learning and discovering new things all the time. Especially about people. People are not nearly as easy to understand as spells, history, or computer systems. People are endlessly complex."

Ten years before, a younger Reg had thought she understood the world and everything in it. Her viewpoint had been very limited. She didn't even know that she had gifts at that point. Now, she had to admit she agreed with Corvin. Each person she met was a new puzzle to be solved and, even when she thought she had them all worked out, she would find out something new, or they would surprise her with something completely unexpected. It wasn't just diversity, it was individuality. No two people were even close to being the same.

"She really loved Patty."

"I could see that," Corvin agreed. "But if she cared for Patty so much, then why couldn't she help? Why not at least try to be more helpful? If she loved her friend and didn't believe that she died of a drug overdose like the police are suggesting, then why didn't she jump at the chance to prove it? Why wasn't she at least happy that someone was trying to find out what had happened?"

"She was. She just... isn't the kind of person who can accept help from others. She can't trust anyone else."

"She doesn't need to. She just needs to be open to finding out new things. To take a little chance to see what we can come up with."

"That's not a little chance. It's making herself vulnerable."

Corvin scoffed at this. "She has no idea about my... curse."

"I don't mean that kind of vulnerability. I mean... any time you open up to someone or reveal a weakness, you are making yourself vulnerable to being hurt by them. People like Chelsea have been hurt so many times by so many different people; there's no way she's going to make herself vulnerable to you. A stranger. Someone who just showed up out of the blue demanding answers about someone she loved."

"You don't know anything about her history. Unless you were able to read a lot more about her than I thought you were."

"She's very careful about not revealing her thoughts and feelings. Not the kind of person who is easy to read. But that doesn't mean I don't understand what she's thinking and feeling."

Corvin was silent as he navigated his way out of the neighborhood's winding streets.

"I hope that the last one isn't as bad as Patty," Reg said, nudging him to tell her something about the third victim.

"I can't say you're going to be happy about it."

Reg let out a sigh. She really wasn't enjoying herself. She had always thought it would be cool to be a private investigator like she saw on TV. She knew the portrayals were unrealistic and romanticized, but she had still thought it would be an interesting profession. But, like Corvin, she was not enjoying the interviews and didn't feel they were getting anything out of them.

Shouldn't they have already had an "aha" moment? Have turned up something important? How could they go through two full interviews without finding any similarities that pointed to the culprit or means of death?

Were they really just coincidences? Could Corvin be wrong about the connection between them?

"I'm not wrong," Corvin growled.

Reg glanced over at him and didn't bother to respond. If he was going to get inside her head without her invitation, then he couldn't very well complain about what he found there. She hadn't expressed any doubts out loud, hadn't intended to share her private thoughts with him.

The next neighborhood was another nice suburban one. Green lawns, kids bicycling down the sidewalk, single-family bungalows with white picket fences. Not exactly Reg's scene, but she could understand the allure. Wasn't that what everyone was looking for? Spouse, kids, and a white picket fence? The American dream?

But something had apparently happened there to make it someone's nightmare instead of their dream. Some mother or father had been taken from the family, breaking it forever.

Corvin was checking house numbers, driving slowly down the street and, eventually, found the one he was looking for. He pulled in at the curb.

They approached the house together. Reg had a growing sense of dread in the pit of her stomach. She had faced two of these deaths already. Deaths that made no sense and had no apparent connection, and had just struck like lightning out of nowhere. How was a family supposed to prevent something like that? How could anyone protect their families from every danger?

Corvin paused before the door, apparently steeling himself for what they were about to face. And he knew better than she did what they were about to encounter. He rang the doorbell.

CHAPTER FIFTEEN

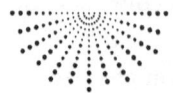

*T*hey waited, listening to footsteps and muffled voices inside before someone finally came to the door. A barking, yipping dog hurried to the front door and window and scurried back and forth, being as menacing as possible, scratching the door, jumping up and down, and making a considerable racket.

"That's enough! Shut up! Here, lock him up," a male voice instructed. "Get him out of here."

After another minute, the door opened, and a tall, thin, balding man peered out at them.

"You're Hunter?" he asked.

Corvin nodded.

The man hesitated about letting them in, looking at Reg and then back at Corvin again. He must know something about Corvin's nature, making him reluctant to let such a creature into his home.

"I suppose," he said finally. He opened the door wider and let them in.

The house was tidier than either of the others, though it was obvious that a busy family lived there. There were different sizes of shoes on the shelves at the door. A few scattered toys and books in the living room. The smells of cooking food wafted from the kitchen. The man gestured for them to sit down, and neither had to clear a space for themselves on the couch.

"I'm Gary Shoop," he introduced himself, offering his hand to Reg but not to Corvin. "Suzie, my wife, will be out in a moment after she deals with Minnie."

He cleared his throat and sat down on an easy chair. Reg instantly recognized the "dad chair." Gary Shoop's favorite seat, which no one else was allowed to use. A recliner with a newspaper and iPad on the side table, a cup holder for his coffee or beer, the seat cushion well-worn with an indentation his butt slipped into whenever he sat down.

Gary looked as though he had realized too late that he should be acting as the host. "Uh—I should get you something to drink. Coffee? Beer?"

Corvin and Reg both declined.

"Honey," Gary called out to his wife as she apparently returned from shutting the barking Minnie in a room somewhere. "Would you bring out coffee for our guests? And some of those cookies?"

Reg tried to protest, but he waved her to silence. Clearly *he* wanted coffee and cookies, whether everybody else did or not.

In a few minutes, Suzie Shoop bustled into the living room. With coffee service, including a plate of store-bought chocolate chip cookies. She set the tray down and looked at Reg and Corvin, pushing her gray and blond hair back over one ear.

"Hi. I'm Suzie. Help yourself."

"Thank you," Reg said politely, but she didn't make any move to. Corvin didn't either. A shadow passed over his face, and she knew he was remembering the poisoned drink he had been served at his club, a gift from an anonymous member. Corvin could have been killed, and had certainly been sick, taken away in an ambulance. He wasn't about to drink anything served to him by strangers. Especially strangers who had refused to shake his hand.

Reg gave a little nod to indicate her support. Suzie raised her brows, looking disappointed that neither of them was interested in the refreshments. She started to sit down in the chair closest to the couch, but Gary motioned her over to a chair that would put her on his other side, protected from Corvin. Suzie hesitated for a moment, then took his suggestion and sat farther away from them. Not far enough that she would have been able to avoid Corvin's pheromones if he had been trying to seduce her. But he wasn't, so she was safe.

Gary sat up and leaned over the coffee service. He put a mug in the cup holder of his recliner and scowled at the cookies. "I wanted the other ones."

Suzie shook her head. "What other ones?"

"The chocolate ones."

"I don't have any chocolate cookies."

"Yes, we do. They were right next to this bag."

She continued to shake her head.

"Did the kids eat them all? I told them they were only allowed to have one per day. If they're all gone…"

"I don't know what you're talking about. We didn't have any chocolate cookies. Just these. They're chocolate chip," she pointed out, as if he might be confused on that point.

"I want the other ones," he told her irritably. He got up and went into the kitchen himself, not waiting for her to comply and serve him.

They could hear him rummaging in the kitchen. He came to the kitchen doorway where he could see his wife but was out of Reg's view line. "These ones." He shook a paper bag.

"Those aren't cookies," Suzie protested. "But go ahead and have some. You're so concerned about other people eating them before you get the chance…"

"I just don't want the kids eating too many of them. They'll be up all night puking."

Gary returned to the living room with another small plate to add to the coffee service. Small chocolate balls, like the truffles that Sarah had brought to Reg. Gary offered them to Reg and Corvin with a quick motion, not actually giving them enough time to take one if they wanted to. But that was fine, because neither of them wanted one.

"These are addictive," Gary told them, putting the small plate down on the table and popping one of the truffles into his mouth. "You wouldn't believe how good they are. And you can't just stop at one…"

Suzie leaned over and snagged one as well. She didn't gobble it, but nibbled at the small ball of chocolate, making it last as long as possible.

"That's why I told the kids they're only allowed to have one per day," Gary told them defensively. "I don't want them getting sick. They don't know when to stop."

"How many kids do you have?" Reg asked.

"Four. Three," Gary corrected himself, and swallowed. "You know about Andy."

Suzie looked down, avoiding looking at them. Her eyes were glassy. Withheld tears. Reg felt sadness, but was surprised by its shallowness. Or maybe the Shoops were just really good at keeping their feelings to themselves. Some people masked well and were able to shield themselves against psychic snooping.

"I was very sorry to read about Andy," Corvin said. "Such a tragic loss. And very sudden…?"

"Yes. Sometimes with kids, you don't really have any warning. They get sick so quickly and sometimes don't know themselves when something is wrong. They're not attuned to listening to their own bodies yet."

"Do they know what it was?" Reg asked.

Gary and Suzie both shook their heads.

"Maybe something will come up in the autopsy," Gary said. "When they came for him… they said maybe something like SIDS, but in older kids. Usually, once they're past a year old, they're not at risk for Sudden Infant Death anymore, but I guess heart problems can come out of nowhere no matter how old you are. They said that maybe he had a heart defect of some kind. It just wasn't discovered when he was born. They don't always find that kind of thing. They just listen to the heart with a stethoscope and, if everything sounds good, that's it. There can be a lot of defects that you can't hear on a stethoscope."

Suzie shook her head slowly. "He didn't have any warning

signs, but they said that's how it is sometimes. The kid doesn't slow down very much or act sick, but a problem with the rhythm can just stop the heart like that…"

"I'm so sorry," Reg commiserated. "Did he just die in his sleep? Maybe you don't want to talk about it. It's kind of rude of me to ask."

"That's why you're here, isn't it?" Gary asked. "You said something about other people who had died." He looked at Corvin. "You thought it might be some kind of pattern. What does that mean? A virus? An epidemic?"

"We don't know yet," Corvin said vaguely. "It's possible. Why don't you tell us what you can about Andy? If he had any symptoms leading up to his death, and how it happened… it's probably easier if you just tell us what you can than us asking you questions and interrupting you."

CHAPTER SIXTEEN

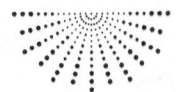

*G*ary and Suzie looked at each other, communicating without words as they decided how to proceed. Maybe they had discussed it before Reg and Corvin had come. Or maybe they were just communicating it now, with facial expressions or the kind of telepathy that develops between people in a close relationship. Reg couldn't catch any exchanged thoughts, but that didn't mean they weren't there. Sometimes people were just not on her wavelength.

Apparently, they decided that Gary should be the one to tell the story. Presumably, he was the one less likely to break down and succumb to his grief.

"I don't think there was anything in the days ahead that could have warned us that something was going on. We've gone over it and over it, trying to think if there was something we should have noticed, something we could have done. But if there was anything, it was very mild... maybe a bit pale, irritable. Kids get like that when they're fighting a bug."

Corvin nodded. "Did he... pass in his sleep, or...?"

"No. We were out at the park. Had a family picnic and some playtime. The kids were playing some outdoor games. We have this little kit with a frisbee, ring-toss, and some other lawn games. Andy came back over to where we were sitting at the picnic table and said that he was hot and tired. We gave him a drink and told him to rest for a few minutes until he felt better. He put his head down on the table and fell asleep." Gary swallowed. "We thought it was so cute."

"But he didn't get up again," Suzie contributed. "I shook him after an hour or so to see if he wanted to go play with the others. And… he was gone."

Reg shook her head at the story. At least it had not been violent or painful. But it must have been such a shock to have him playing with his siblings one minute and then the next, gone without warning.

"He hadn't been hit with the ball," Gary said. "They hadn't been roughhousing. He hadn't even been running that much. I think he was tired before that."

"Where are the other kids?" Reg asked. The house was too quiet for them to be at home. She would have heard something from them. The TV, computers, children playing or arguing, all of those sounds were missing.

"They're at my brother's," Gary explained. "We didn't want them around for this discussion. Interrupting with every little thing, or being exposed to…" Gary raised his brows and nodded slightly at Corvin. "We have to keep their welfare in mind."

Reg cleared her throat. She knew it was unlikely that Corvin would ever prey upon a child, but she couldn't say so with one hundred percent certainty. He had, after all, been the one to steal Marta Jessup's powers from her before she was even born.

"And none of them noticed anything?" Reg asked. "Sometimes kids notice something, but they don't tell adults because they don't think they'll be believed, or they think that the adults know better than they do."

"Our kids did not know anything was wrong," Gary said firmly.

"Even afterward," Reg pressed.

"Even afterward. They didn't know. I'm telling you."

Reg nodded. "Okay," she agreed.

Gary stared at her for a minute, his eyes big black holes, then he finally nodded as if he believed she wasn't trying to accuse his children of something.

"Andy might have been feeling 'off' for a few days?" Corvin asked, returning to the earlier part of the conversation.

They nodded and looked at each other, but neither provided any more details.

"Is there anything that had changed recently? Diet, a new friend, something going on at school? Anything? Did he seem anxious?"

"No. Nothing had changed," Gary said. They both shook their heads. "Everything was just the same as it always was. No big changes. Don't you think we've racked our brains and gone over and over this? There's no way to explain what happened or for us to have prevented it."

"We're not accusing you," Reg assured them. "We're just hoping to find some kind of connection between the three deaths. It seems so strange that there should be three unexplained deaths like this so close together in the magical community of Black Sands."

Corvin looked at Reg after she said that, one eyebrow raised to ask her whether that meant she was fully on his side now and believed that there was something strange going on and not just a coincidence. Reg shrugged slightly with one shoulder and didn't give him an answer. Not yet.

"How have your other children been?" Reg asked. "I mean… has everyone else felt okay? No one else is… pale or irritable, more tired than usual… anything?"

"Andy's death has affected all of us. So yes, of course, we're all out of sorts and getting on each other's nerves when we should be drawing closer together," Gary admitted. His jaw was clenched and his eyes flashed. This was clearly not something he wanted to explore any further. He was ready for them to leave and, in another moment, would likely be herding them toward the door.

"That kind of thing happens when you have a death in the family," Suzie contributed. "People all react differently and have to work through it at different rates and in different ways." She looked at her husband and swallowed. "A lot of marriages don't survive the loss of a child. It's a very difficult time."

"I'm sure it is," Reg agreed. But they had, she thought, missed the point. They were too focused on blame and not knowing why Andy had died. "I just wondered whether anyone else has been sick."

"No one is sick."

"Heart defects aren't contagious," Gary pointed out. "None of the other children are in danger."

"You don't know for sure that it was a heart defect."

"But that's what the doctors said. They would have to investigate further, but they figured that's what it was. Just a chance thing, something we never could have known."

"But some kinds of heart defects are genetic," Corvin said. "Did they look at any of the other children? Test them for anything? Viruses? Genes? What they ate? Did they do any kind of investigation?"

"No." Gary shook his head. He was pretty pale himself. He and Suzie looked at each other, trying valiantly to keep up with Corvin's questions and still stay in sync with each other, determined not to show any weakness or difference of opinions. "They didn't think that it was anything the other children could have gotten. They weren't worried about anyone else. Do you know something? Or are you just here to make waves and to make us feel bad?"

"We don't know," Reg admitted. "That's what we're trying to figure out. If there is anything that we should be concerned about. Because three people died, not just Andy. If it was just one person... that would be different."

"We don't even know those other people," Suzie said. "We didn't have anything to do with them. They didn't have anything to do with us. I think... it was just a coincidence. I know you want to put something sinister on it... but I don't think there is anything to tie them together. It's just a weird coincidence. It probably happens all the time, but you noticed because of social media. We hear more about things happening in the community and the world now. Things that you wouldn't have known about other years. It would have gone unremarked."

She sighed and shook her head. She rubbed her neck as if it were stiff, then leaned forward and took another truffle from the plate. "You really should try these. They are so lovely. So many truffles are heavy and rich, but these ones are light and sweet, just the right combination of ingredients. And you can get some of them with different herbs or other ingredients. To help you stay awake, go to sleep, or focus…" She shrugged. "These are just the normal ones, but I want to try all the others too."

She ate the truffle in a couple of dainty bites, then braced her hands on her knees as if she had an unpleasant task to perform. "And now… I think it's time for you to go. I'm sorry we haven't been able to help you. Good luck with your investigation, but I'm afraid we don't know anything else that will help you. It's just… it was just fate that Andy was taken from us when he was. It's just the way that things turned out. We couldn't have stopped it. No one could have."

Reg stood up and so did Corvin. They both took one last look around the room, trying to spot that *one thing* that would tie the investigation together. There had to be one thing that made them all similar. But other than vague recollections that the victims might have been tired, pale, or irritable did little to help. They could be remembering wrong. Filling in extra details because it seemed like there should be some answer there. They wanted it to make sense. They wanted it to be natural causes, to be something that was beyond anyone's control. Just enough to hint that they might have been sick, but not enough that anyone could have done anything about it.

CHAPTER SEVENTEEN

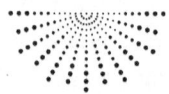

*C*orvin dropped Reg at home after they were finished with
the interviews. Neither of them had very much to say in
the car. What was there to say? Neither of them could find a clue
that would point them to how the deaths were related if, indeed,
they were. They had conducted three interviews, and three sets of
interviewees had not had any suggestions as to why their loved one
had died. No preexisting conditions were known, no mysterious
new person in their lives. No enemy. No mention of anyplace they
might have known each other from. There were no lines they could
draw between the three victims. Other than the manner and timing
of their deaths.

They just kept running into brick walls.

"We'll sleep on it," Reg told Corvin, trying to sound confident
and lighthearted. "Think about it before you go to bed, tell your
brain that you want to solve it while you're sleeping, and then go to
sleep. Then your unconscious will sort it out and in the morning…" She trailed off and shrugged, looking out the side window
so he wouldn't see the discouragement in her eyes.

"When has that ever worked for you before?" Corvin
demanded.

"Oh, all the time. You've never done that? It works brilliantly."

Corvin stared straight ahead at the road before the car and didn't comment.

"Okay… it doesn't always work," Reg confessed. "Sometimes you aren't any farther ahead in the morning than when you went to sleep. But it's worth a try, isn't it?"

"You don't think I've been trying the last couple of days?"

"I don't think you've been sleeping."

"Well, that's true enough," Corvin admitted.

"Then try it for one night. Get plenty of sleep and tell yourself you'll know the solution when you get up in the morning."

"Fine," he said flatly. "We'll both do that."

Reg didn't think he had very much confidence that it would work.

But sometimes, it did.

Corvin pulled over in front of Sarah's house. "Shall I walk you in?"

Reg looked at him. It was the first attempt he had made at getting her alone, something that he was usually trying to do all the time. But he didn't even look at her. It was like he didn't even know he had said it. It was just part of his goodbye routine.

"No, thanks," Reg got out of the car. She had several things to do and wasn't going to spend any time worrying about the fact that Corvin wasn't paying her the attention he usually did. He had a lot on his plate if he was going to solve the mystery behind the three deaths. And he needed sleep. "Talk to you tomorrow."

"Okay."

Reg shut the car door and walked to the back gate and into the backyard without looking back. She would be able to hear or feel him if he followed her into the yard. Instead, she heard his car engine rev once, and then he peeled away from the curb and drove swiftly away. The sound of the car engine and tires faded to nothing.

Reg was left with a strange, hollow feeling that she wasn't sure what to call. Loneliness? Did she miss Corvin? Miss the little games he was always playing?

Maybe she was just hungry.

* * *

Reg knocked on the back door of the big house later that evening, still feeling alone and out of sorts. Sarah always told her to just go straight in but, after being raised to never enter a home without an invitation, Reg couldn't quite find it in her heart to do so. She knocked, then opened the screen door and poked her head in.

"It's Reg! Are you home, Sarah?"

Of course, she already knew that Sarah was home. She could feel her presence in the house, like a little ticking alarm clock across the room. She listened for an answer, then raised her voice and repeated the call.

"Sarah? Do you have a minute for tea?"

Eventually, she heard some thumping around upstairs. Probably Sarah hadn't even heard her call. Reg went to the stairs and shouted up them.

"Sarah?"

"Who's that?" Sarah came out of the upstairs hallway and looked down the stairs. "Oh, Reg. What are you doing here?"

Reg hesitated. "Are you busy? Were you in the middle of something?"

Sarah looked back over her shoulder as if she weren't sure. "Oh... no, nothing that can't wait. How about a cup of tea?"

"Yeah. That would be nice," Reg agreed.

Sarah descended the stairs and they both returned to the kitchen, where Sarah put the kettle on and moved the rest of the tea things to the table so that Reg could make her choice of tea and add the appropriate heaping teaspoons of sugar. Reg preferred the commercial teabags to Sarah's homemade mixes, which generally tasted awful no matter how much sugar Reg added to them.

"How has your day been?" Sarah inquired.

"Well, it was fine. I was out with Corvin, trying to find out what we could about the recent deaths in the community."

"Oh?" Sarah did not react. "That sounds interesting."

CHAPTER EIGHTEEN

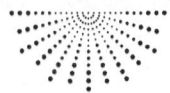

*R*eg stared at Sarah in disbelief. She should have immediately launched into a lecture about how Reg should not be anywhere near Corvin and needed to look out for him. She certainly shouldn't be getting into the car with him alone and giving up any independence she had to sit beside him in an enclosed space.

And even if she didn't have any warnings about Corvin—maybe by now she had given up on Reg ever taking her advice on the matter and had decided to just ignore any stupidity on Reg's part—she should still have shown some reaction to the mention of the deaths in the community. She must know of the members who had died just as much as, if not more than, Corvin. She had been in the community at least as long as Corvin had and knew all of the ancient families and their descendants.

Or she could at least do what everyone else had done and say that she didn't think there was anything to the deaths. They were just sad affairs, natural deaths, unconnected. Nothing for Reg and Corvin to probe any further.

Concerned by this change from Sarah's usual behavior, Reg watched her bustle around the kitchen, shuffling through various ingredients to add to the tea tray or get out for supper, and picking up the kettle when it started to whistle.

Sarah looked at the kettle in her hand momentarily as though it were a foreign object before recognizing it and remembering what she was supposed to be doing.

Sarah had not been this vague and forgetful since she had lost her emerald necklace. With it restored to her and some pixie magic, she had returned to her previous health and vigor.

"Are you feeling okay, Sarah?"

"Oh, yes. Don't you worry about me. I'm just fine. Every day above ground is a good day."

Reg hoped that Sarah was getting more out of life than that. Sarah had always seemed to enjoy life. She had a large group of friends and acquaintances and did a lot more socially than Reg.

"You're a little pale," Reg suggested, studying her friend's face.

And her aura. Something was wrong with her aura. It was dimmer than usual. Maybe a little green? What did that mean? Did that mean that Sarah was sick? What if she were suffering the same affliction as the other three magical practitioners whose families she and Corvin had visited? What if this was Reg's one chance to identify the illness and get Sarah the help she needed?

"Have you had anything different to eat today?" she pressed. "Or have you been with anyone else who has been sick lately? Anyone connected with the three people who died?"

Sarah scowled. "I told you, Reg, there is nothing wrong. Don't be silly. Have your tea." She motioned to Reg's empty mug.

Reg picked up one of the tea bags from the basket in front of her and hung it over the edge of the mug. "Could I get some water?"

Sarah stared at her, then looked down at the kettle in her hand. She shook her head in confusion, then poured the boiling water carefully into Reg's cup. She put it back down on the stove before realizing that she needed water in her mug too, and filled it.

"Have you been feeling poorly?" Reg stared down at the tea as she stirred sugar into it and stirred the tea bag around.

"I'm tired," Sarah admitted. "But that's all right. Tell me you've never been tired!"

"Of course I have," Reg laughed. "I'm just worried because of what's been happening."

Sarah sat down at the table and picked up a cookie, which she munched on while they talked. "Worried about what?"

"With the people who had died. They didn't really have many symptoms ahead of time, just pale, tired, irritable…"

"That could describe half the population at least half the time. You can't think that everyone who is tired is going to die."

"No. But I'm concerned about my friends. You seem a little… off."

"I told you, I'm tired," Sarah snapped. She dipped her cookie in her tea and then took a bite. "After as many years as I've lived on this earth, it's perfectly reasonable that I would be tired sometimes. You're the one who spends half of your day sleeping."

Even though Reg realized that Sarah's irritability was probably being triggered by something other than Reg's questions, Sarah's comment was still hurtful. She was just trying to ensure a friend's welfare.

She sipped her tea and was about to reach for a cookie when she changed her mind. If Sarah were getting sick, anything around her might have been contaminated. It could be a virus, bacteria, poison, potion, or a magical curse. It could be attached to anything Sarah touched, something she had eaten or drunk, or even just in the air. Reg breathed shallowly and decided she would not be finishing her tea. She kept stirring it, giving her hands something to do and making it look like she was drinking tea with Sarah, but she would not drink another drop.

Should she call Corvin? Let him know that Sarah might be another victim? She wished that they had something to go on. She couldn't very well call an ambulance or take Sarah to the hospital with the suggestion that something might be wrong. Still, she only had the vague symptoms of being tired and cranky. Tired and cranky wasn't exactly emergency-room-worthy.

"What did you do today? Did you go out with any of your friends?"

"No, I don't have the energy to go out right now. I had a nap. Watched some TV. I don't normally just lie around the house, but today I just... couldn't get myself moving."

"Do you need anything done around here?"

Sarah shook her head. "Like what?"

"I just thought... if you don't have the energy, there might be things that you need done around the house that you can't do for yourself right now. I can help if you need me to cook you some soup or do some cleaning? I used to do some elder care, you know. I'm pretty good at helping out around the house."

"Are you calling me old?"

"No—"

"Feeble?"

"Sarah!" Reg protested. "You said you didn't have any energy to do anything today; you're not feeling very well. So I'm just asking if there is anything I can do for you. Do you need some help with something?"

"I will be just fine, thank you very much. Now if that is all, you're making me tired. Maybe you'd better go home and make sure you are prepared for your evening sessions."

Another arrow struck a tender place. Reg wasn't someone who made friends easily, and Sarah had been a good friend since Reg had first moved to Black Sands, from the very first day. Despite their ages, she felt closer to Sarah than anyone else in Black Sands. She had never been shooed out of the house like that before. And for Sarah to take offense that Reg had offered to help her out... it just didn't seem fair. What was Reg supposed to do? Stay away when Sarah wasn't feeling well? Ignore her and her problems? Act like she didn't care?

She guessed that what she was supposed to do was what Sarah asked. Go back to the cottage so that Sarah could get some rest. Maybe that was all that she needed. It was probably nothing. She probably just had a bit of the flu or was tired out from social functions.

It wasn't anything. It didn't mean she was dying of whatever had killed the others.

CHAPTER NINETEEN

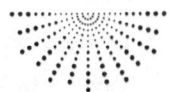

*S*he did her best to take Sarah's advice and just look at her schedule and prepare for her evening appointments. But she couldn't. There was no way to know whether Sarah was on the verge of succumbing to whatever evil had killed the others. She couldn't waste a single minute of her available time. Did she have another day? Only one night? Only a few hours? She couldn't just ignore the possibility that Sarah was in grave danger and go on with her life as usual.

She called the people who had appointments and apologized that something else had come up and she couldn't see them. She would need to reschedule for another time.

None of them was nasty about it, and there weren't any birthday parties or other events that couldn't be put off. Just routine readings and forays into the unseen world. They understood that Reg could not have foreseen that a close family member would fall ill—although one of them did joke that, as a psychic, she should have known that. They were all amenable to being rescheduled to a more convenient night.

With her business obligations out of the way, Reg called Marta. She pushed away the nagging doubts about not putting the needed time into her business. Her bread and butter. But relationships were supposed to come first, weren't they? Friendships and family members were more important than one night of work. She would make it up in the following days and wouldn't have lost anything.

"Hello? Reg?" Marta's voice intruded on Reg's thoughts. She looked at the phone in her hand and realized she had called Marta, and then had zoned out and not heard Marta pick up.

"Oh, sorry. I just got distracted by something."

"What's up?"

"Nothing. Well, that's not true. I wondered whether we could get together. I want to talk something through with you. I don't know. I need a sounding board. Someone to tell me whether I'm being crazy or…"

"Probably being crazy," Marta said cheerfully. "But I suppose there always is a 'something else.' Your timing is pretty good. I just clocked out and am getting changed and ready to go home. Do you want me to come over there?"

"No…" Reg didn't want Sarah to see Marta coming and going and to come to the conclusion that it was something to do with her or that they were doing something covert. Which they were. She wanted to be free to discuss the situation with Marta without the possibility of Sarah breezing in to say hello or to add another appointment to Reg's calendar. "Do you want to go out for coffee? I'd like to just relax and chat for a while…"

"Sure. The Witches' Brew?" Marta suggested their usual coffee shop.

"That would be great. Are you going to go straight over there, or do you need to go home first?"

"I can go straight over. I'm getting in my civvies now, so I can relax and just have a coffee with my gal at the end of the day."

"Okay. I'll see you over there in a few minutes, then."

Reg was relieved to be doing something. She knew that, as she had discussed with Corvin, they had nothing to take to the police. There wasn't any evidence of foul play. There wasn't anything to tie the deaths or the people together. But she could talk to Marta informally and see if there were something they could develop together. There had to be something she could do to move the investigation forward, even if the police couldn't officially take it on.

After she got off the phone, Reg petted Starlight and gave him his dinner, and then headed out to The Witches' Brew.

Corvin always made fun of Reg for the fancy coffees she loved at The Witches' Brew. He was a black coffee or espresso guy, and the sweet treats Reg enjoyed made him grimace. But Reg could have regular coffee at home—especially since she had the fancy new machine now—if she went out for coffee, it should be an *experience.*

Marta was there ahead of her and had staked out a booth, which was good because the after-dinner crowd was already starting to show up and, before long, there wouldn't be any free seats.

They greeted each other, and Reg took Marta's order so that she could stay at the table. Since she had just gotten off of work, she was having a sandwich as well as her cup of coffee. Plain old Joe, Reg was disappointed to note. Marta was watching her figure, which was probably why she was avoiding the sugary drinks. But what was the point in coming to a specialty coffee shop for plain coffee?

The barista prepared everything for Reg. She motioned to the sample stand beside the register. "Free sample of Mystical Morsels with every purchase," she offered. "These things sell like hotcakes. If you haven't tried them, you should."

Reg took a couple and put them on Marta's plate. If she wasn't having sugar in her coffee, she might as well have a modest dessert. There couldn't be more than a couple of grams of sugar in the morsels.

She sat across from Marta and took her coffee, pushing the tray with the rest of the purchase to Marta.

"How was your day?"

"Well, about the same as usual. Either dead boring or dealing with idiots making bad choices."

Reg chuckled. She imagined there were a lot of those.

"Oh, truffles!" Marta pounced on the chocolates. Her eyes shone. "These are so good. Have you tried one?"

"No, not yet. Sarah brought some over. I'll have them later." Reg frowned. She didn't remember seeing them on the counter where she had left them. Had Sarah taken them back? Put them into the cupboard or fridge, so Starlight wouldn't get at them? Or had Starlight taken them? He sometimes liked to push things off the counter or drag them off to play with. And those little chocolate balls would probably be fun to chase around the cottage and lose under the furniture. Hopefully, he hadn't eaten any, because chocolate was not good for cats. Or was that dogs? Or both?

"Have one," Marta motioned to the truffles Reg had put on her plate. "You really should try them."

"I'm just going to have my coffee right now. There's plenty of chocolate and sugar in that. I don't want so much that it keeps me up after two or three in the morning."

Marta rolled her eyes. But she seemed happy enough to keep both morsels for herself. She nibbled at one of them, closing her eyes to savor it. She popped the rest in her mouth and let it melt, giving a sigh of pleasure.

"So… what did you want to talk about?"

Reg shrugged. "I just thought we should get together. It's been a little while."

"You didn't just want to get together. So what's going on?"

"I thought you didn't have any psychic powers."

Marta grinned. "I don't need psychic powers to read you. I just know you. And you don't just call me up out of the blue to chat. You want something."

Reg took a long drink of her Hazelnut Hocus Pocus Latte. She put it down on the table in front of her and tried to decide how to approach the topic. She had thought that she would be able to ease into it, just casually discuss the things she had learned from Corvin and the interviewees, and then mention Sarah's possible symptoms.

But maybe it was better that it was all out in the open from the start. Especially if Sarah's life *was* in danger. Wasn't it best to tackle it as quickly as possible?

"It's just… Doesn't it seem strange to you that three people in the same community would just die—for no apparent reason—the same week?"

"Well... no. It happens all the time. Like I said before. You hear about three musicians or celebrities that all died in the same month, or in January of the same year, and you start predicting that it is going to be a really bad year and other celebrities are going to die. And it's just because you heard of them all around the same time. There isn't really anything connecting them except your brain catching on to something that it thought was a cluster or pattern."

"That isn't all it is," Reg insisted.

Marta raised her brows.

"It isn't," Reg repeated. "If you talk to all the families, they all say the same thing. Everything was normal, except maybe the person was a little more tired or pale or a little bit 'off,' and then they died."

"Well, what do you expect? They will try to find a reason for the person's death. They're going to grab at anything they can. Everybody is tired, Reg. Everybody gets cranky sometimes. It doesn't mean anything."

"But I just talked to Sarah, and she's..."

CHAPTER TWENTY

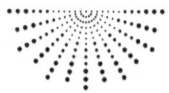

*M*arta was looking across the coffee shop at something. Reg turned to see.

Corvin.

What was he doing there? Did he want to wreck everything? He had already told Reg there was no point in his talking to Marta because she wouldn't have anything to do with him. Reg smacked her forehead with the heel of her hand. "What's *he* doing here?"

"Looking for you, I'd say."

Corvin had indeed spotted Reg from across the room and was now walking toward her.

She saw him realize that Marta was sitting there as well, and there was an infinitesimal pause as he tried to decide whether to proceed. Still, he kept walking toward them, exuding confidence. Even if he didn't actually feel it.

"Reg, fancy finding you here," he said casually. "What a nice surprise."

He slid into the bench seat beside her. They weren't touching, but she could feel his body heat. And if he turned on the charm, she would feel it even more.

"Marta," he acknowledged with a nod. "Or I should say, Detective Jessup."

She had told him that they were not friendly anymore, and Corvin needed to address her formally.

Marta nodded and showed no reaction to his presence. Reg was flummoxed. She had expected fireworks.

Corvin turned his attention to Reg. "You're usually doing evening readings about this time, aren't you?"

"I had other things to do. Talking to Marta, for one."

"Ah."

"She was just telling me about Sarah," Marta said. "What about Sarah, Reg?"

Reg had to pull her focus back to Marta and her question. She couldn't understand why Marta was suddenly being so casual and accepting of Corvin's presence. Had they made up and neither of them had bothered to tell Reg?

But Corvin's eyes were on Reg, wide and questioning, and Reg was reading that he was just as baffled as she was. They hadn't made up. But Reg focused on the question and tried to get back on track.

"I just saw Sarah," she found herself explaining to Corvin rather than Marta. He would understand her, believe her, and realize that something was wrong. "She's... unfocused. Forgetful. She's pale and tired and out of sorts. I'm worried."

He rubbed his whiskered chin. "Hmm."

"Nothing to worry about," Marta assured them. "Who doesn't feel like that sometimes?"

"But you didn't talk to these other families today," Reg argued, "If those are symptoms of an illness or poisoning or a spell... then we might not have very long to act. The families said, 'the last few days.' Their family members had only been sick—pale, out of sorts, tired—for a few days, and then they just died without any other warning. I don't want to go over to Sarah's tomorrow or the next day and find her dead!"

"I think that's an overreaction," Marta said firmly. "You are not thinking it through clearly and logically. You're just reacting emotionally. Like when kids work themselves up to be scared by telling ghost stories or talking about burglars or the man with the hook."

"Or the Cabal of the Withered Paw?" Reg challenged.

Marta looked uncomfortable. "Okay, that turned out to be true. Or at least, someone wanted to resurrect the old legend and make it real. But hysteria over stories and legends makes it real. It scares you, but it isn't necessarily true. You've tied together three disparate events and are trying to make them significant. They aren't."

"Corvin and I think they are," Reg said, looking at Corvin and meeting his eyes. Assuring him that now she was finally on the same page with him. She believed the deaths were related and that there could be more. If they didn't figure out what was killing people, they could lose Sarah and who knew how many other practitioners.

"So this is you," Marta said, looking at Corvin with her head cocked slightly. "I might have known that's where it came from."

"Have you ever known me to make something like this up?" Corvin demanded. "When have I ever suggested there was a threat when there wasn't? You remember about the draugar, don't you? Reg and I were right about that, too. We could both feel what the Witch Doctor was doing, how his power was growing. And we were right. And about the cabal. And when Reg has come to you about a poisoning, or you went to her about the attacks at the harbor. We're not making this stuff up. We just saw it before anyone else."

"I don't think you're right in this case." Marta took another sip of her coffee and pushed her plate away. "I need to get home. I will see you guys later." She stood up and picked up her purse. "Have fun, kids. Don't do anything I wouldn't do."

She walked off, stopping at the register to wish the barista a nice day and to grab another truffle.

CHAPTER TWENTY-ONE

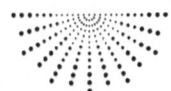

*I*s it just me," Corvin contemplated, "or is everyone behaving a little bit... not like themselves lately?"

Reg sighed. "Something is wrong."

"It is, isn't it?"

"She didn't even turn a hair when you showed up and sat at our table. She didn't say anything about you being *persona non grata* at the Black Sands police department. She acted like you were anyone else. Not... you."

"So, what's going on?"

"I don't know." Reg shook her head. She had a few swallows of her coffee.

"It was *her*, wasn't it?"

Reg blinked, trying to understand what he was saying. "You mean... it was her and not just someone imitating her? Some kind of skin walker or impostor?"

"Yes. Exactly."

"Well... yes. It *felt* like her. I didn't get any weird mental shifts or anything. She didn't miss anything obvious or say the wrong thing. It was just... that her emotions were off. Wrong. And for her to just walk away like that..." Reg looked in the direction Marta had departed. "I'm always trying to end conversations with her. She's never the first one to say she has to go. Unless she is actually going on shift. If we have coffee or girls' night out… she's never the first to leave."

"And you don't think that was because of me?"

"No. If she cared, she would have left the minute you got here. She didn't even flinch."

"And the families that we met with today. I didn't want to say anything at the time, but one of the things that I came here to ask you, was… were *they* off? Were their emotions… right?"

Reg shook her head. "Everyone is individual. No two people will react to a death in the family the same way. But all day, I was trying to understand the dynamics. To make sense of why I couldn't feel the grief from them that I expected to. Were they all just that good at masking and shutting themselves off from me? All of them? Even the parents of that little boy?"

"They were still in shock," Corvin suggested.

"Maybe. Yes. That could be it, of course. It was so recent. But… I just don't know. It was like their emotions were… deadened. That something was stopping them from feeling what they should really feel."

"Should?"

"I can't think of another way to put it," Reg apologized. "I know that not everyone feels the same things, with the same intensity, or shows it the same way. But they just *weren't*. They were acting like they were zombies or drugged."

"Or hypnotized."

"Or ensorcelled."

"Yes," Corvin agreed. "But I didn't sense any presence there that shouldn't be."

"That second woman, Chelsea, she didn't know what you were. Didn't believe in the magical world around her or the community that Patty was a part of."

Corvin nodded his agreement.

"But the others, they knew what you are?"

"Yes. Clearly. With a name like Hunter, it's pretty hard to hide the fact."

"Then why did they agree to meet with you? And if they agreed to meet, why wasn't it in a public place? Out in the open where your pheromones couldn't have a concentrated effect? Why didn't they recruit more powerful practitioners to sit in with them to ensure you couldn't do anything to ensorcel them?"

"Not everyone does those things. Some people think that they can withstand my charms." Corvin gave her a little smile.

"Don't you think they should have?" Reg persisted.

"Of course they should if they don't want to be deceived or taken advantage of. But even those who are aware of who I am and the curse that I bear... they don't all believe it or think that I could affect them. People are... more foolhardy than you would like to think. Even within the community, they still don't believe the old legends."

"Something just isn't right," Reg said. "Something about these people is wrong."

"You think they have been bewitched?" Corvin asked. "But it is so widespread and there are no connections we can find between the families. And Sarah. And Marta."

"How would you be able to put a spell on that many different people? People who apparently don't even cross paths?"

"That's an excellent question."

Reg played with her coffee cup, turning it in circles on the table. She looked around at the other patrons of the coffee shop, reaching out her feelings, touching a mind here and there, trying to get a read on the room.

"I want a serious answer," she said. "How would you do that? Could this be something that John has done? To make it so that he has more opportunities to find victims?"

Corvin wouldn't like to have his newly discovered son accused of such a thing but, if Reg were to follow through her train of thought about each of the families they had visited allowing Corvin into the house without any apparent attempts to protect themselves, then that made Corvin and John the most likely suspects.

"I have no idea what John is and is not capable of," Corvin said in a slow, even voice. "I would like to say that no blood of mine would perpetrate such a crime. But Verity did not raise him with the same scruples as he would have if I'd had a hand in it. She was…" Corvin trailed off and shook his head, apparently unable to find the right words. Or words that were appropriate to use in a public place.

"She was twisted up," Reg said. "She'd become… bent up and unnatural. She didn't think she had to follow the rules. Or decided not to."

It wasn't like those who were afflicted with Corvin's condition had to follow a lot of onerous rules or were punished if they did not. The fact that Corvin had, for a time, been shunned by his coven for his improper dealings with Reg was very unusual. He got away with a lot of things that he shouldn't have because the pendulum had swung too far in the opposite direction. Once Corvin had complained about the prejudice against his type and how they should be allowed to operate according to their nature.

But from what Reg had seen, public opinion had shifted so much in the other direction that power drinkers were afforded every possible indulgence and were not dealt with unless they were caught in the very act of consuming a woman's powers without her consent. Even then, Reg had been a little surprised that the tribunal had found against Corvin. Now he was back in favor and actually the leader of the coven that had once shunned him. Too quickly. Far too quickly.

"I will try to approach John on the matter. Circumspectly, of course, so that hopefully… he doesn't see where I am coming from or what I am after."

"You think he would tell you if he'd ensorcelled half the town?"

"We don't know it is that widespread."

Reg raised her brows.

Corvin sighed. "Okay. Yes, it is a significant portion of the magical community, if we are to go by what we saw today. Five different families or people from five different walks of life who seem to be showing the same symptoms… that has to mean that it is widespread."

"Do you think one person could do that?"

"With the right mode of introducing the spell… yes, I think one person could. But they would have to be smart about it. It wouldn't be easy to reach that many different people."

"How would *you* do it?"

CHAPTER TWENTY-TWO

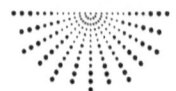

*C*orvin thought about it. He looked at Reg's coffee and Marta's mostly emptied cup, and started to stand. "I need some grease to get these gears running," he explained.

Then he stopped. Reg had been looking around the room at the various other patrons, wondering how many of them might be showing symptoms of the same malady. She stopped and looked back at him sharply, as if he had grabbed her hand and jerked her over to him.

"What?" Reg complained, rubbing the back of her neck. A girl could get whiplash with her attention being grabbed so violently.

"Something like this…" Corvin pointed at Reg's coffee. "Pretty much everyone who comes into this store gets coffee in some form. How hard would it be to contaminate the source?"

"I don't know. Anyone working here could drop something into the grounds or an open carafe. But… Chelsea… you think she would ever come somewhere like this? She couldn't afford it. And this is a witch hangout; you don't see many non-practitioners here."

"But Patty might have taken something home with her. They might have shared a drink." His eyes traveled over the other wares at the ordering counter. "Or a pastry."

He and Reg both said it at the same time, their brains following the same path: "Or a truffle."

They stared at each other.

"Do you really think that's what it is?" Reg asked, breathless.

"Let's go through them one at a time. Clearly, Marta has been eating them." Corvin pointed to a dusting of cocoa left on Marta's plate.

"Yes. And Sarah. She brought me a bag of them. Wanted me to have some. Kept telling me how wonderful they are."

"Okay." Corvin nodded. "Beverley Bartley?"

"Liked to have a snack before bed. They would have something sweet or salty as a treat at the end of the day."

Corvin's eyes were alight. "The roommates? Patty Meiers?"

"I don't know for sure, but there were bags of cookies and such in one of the cupboards. Maybe truffles; I couldn't swear one way or the other. And Chelsea said that one of Patty's favorite things—addictions—was chocolate. So it would make sense."

They both looked at each other, silent, as they thought about Andy Shoop. There was no need to speculate whether the Shoop family had truffles in the house. They had seen them firsthand. Heard Gary Shoop complaining to his wife that he wanted the chocolate cookies, not the ones she had brought out, and had watched him fetch a plate of them from the kitchen.

"Do you think that's it, then?" Reg asked. "Where did these Mystical Morsels come from? I never saw them before I came back from my vacation. Then suddenly… they're everywhere. Everyone is eating them and telling me how wonderful they are."

"You haven't had any?"

Reg shook her head. "I actually don't like truffles."

He stared pointedly at her coffee. "You don't like chocolate truffles?" he repeated in disbelief.

"They're really rich. Give me an upset stomach."

"So you haven't even tasted the Mystical Morsels?"

"No. I was going to. Sarah brought me some, like I said, but I haven't had any yet. And I don't remember them being on the counter when I was there last. Maybe Sarah came back and reclaimed them. If so… she's apparently eating a lot of them."

"So if those are poisoning symptoms, she is definitely being affected. The truffles. Why didn't I think of it before?"

"Do you know who makes them? Where they come from?"

"They showed up at the bakery and the grocery store. Free samples. People usually go on to buy a bag. And then another, and another. They're like those cookies the girls sell. The chocolate mint. Everyone hoards them."

"There are samples here," Reg pointed to the order counter where they were displayed beside the till. "And where else?"

"Most of the establishments I've been to lately have had them out. Someone is putting a lot of money into having them on display."

"It must be a local baker, then. Cook. What do you call it?"

"A chocolatier?" Corvin suggested.

"Yeah. Must be a local chocolatier. Do you know who it is?"

He shook his head. "No, but I can find out."

He went to the counter to order himself a cup of coffee. Reg could see him pointing to the truffles and asking the barista questions, smiling at her and leaning in slightly. The barista got the same cow-like awestruck expression they all got when basking in Corvin's charms.

Corvin returned to the table with his coffee. He sat down. "They've already put out their last samples and thrown the bag away. She said to check with the bakery here in town."

"Gingerbread Lane?"

Corvin grimaced and nodded.

Reg laughed. "You don't like the name?"

"I don't like the association between gingerbread houses and children being lured to their deaths. I don't think it's a particularly sensitive name."

"Were you raised on stories of witches in the forest luring children to their deaths?"

"Many stories have been invented in the magical community about… people with my affliction. Luring children or other innocents to their deaths. Even though we are not known for killing our... targets. Cautionary tales to keep children from trusting friendly little old ladies in the forest or men offering sweet treats."

Reg was sickened at the thought. "Your kind targets children?" she demanded. She had only ever seen Corvin charm women.

"Historically... it has happened. There are laws now that prevent such things. We are only to enchant adults, and only with their consent."

But Reg knew from experience that Corvin didn't always follow the "only with their consent" part of the rule. Did he follow the other rules? Or was he just as happy to target a child who happened to be available? Some boy playing on his own or girl walking home from school by herself. Children might be told not to take treats from strangers, but what about the ice cream man driving around town playing his sickly-sweet tunes? What about free samples offered at the register?

And what about the power drinker who exuded the scent of baking brownies, like John? He seemed particularly equipped to lure an unsuspecting child away from his friends or intended route.

"John's pheromones smell like chocolate," she said aloud.

Corvin shrugged. "Yes. I noticed."

"Could he have something to do with these truffles? Maybe it's his trademark. His way to make his victims vulnerable even before he arrives at the scene. Get them into a chocolate coma, with this reduced emotional state, and then... make his move."

"That seems... like a stretch. John wouldn't need so many targets. There's no need to blanket the whole town with treats when he only needs one..."

"Why stop at one when he could have his pick of nearly any woman in town?"

"That's not the way our kind works. We don't... hoard."

"Maybe not normally, but you don't know how he was raised. Kids who hoard food, it's usually because they were starved as children."

Reg had seen enough cases like that in foster care. She had *been* a case like that. She still kept crackers in her purse, as long as she could keep Ember out of it. She had cupboards and a fridge stuffed so full of food she could never find what she was looking for.

"If Verity was making John share his power with her, he might have been that child who was always hungry and learned to hoard whatever he could for later."

"And you think he would attempt to bring the whole town under his thrall so that he would always have his next victim on hand? So that he would never go hungry?" Corvin challenged.

"It's possible," Reg insisted.

"Yes," Corvin agreed flatly. "But I don't think it's very likely."

"Well… I guess we should get over to Gingerbread Lane and find out."

Corvin looked at the large, shiny watch on his wrist. Who still wore watches like that? It seemed like anyone Reg knew who still wore a watch instead of just checking the time on their phone was wearing a fitness watch. Something that counted their steps, monitored their heart rate, and communicated vital statistics with their phone.

"They're closed."

Reg's heart fell. "Then we'll have to wait until tomorrow."

"*Early* tomorrow," Corvin advised. "Bakers are up before the sun, and they'll open their doors for the breakfast rush before eight."

Reg had seen the kind of hours Erin kept. It was disgusting the way that she got up for her day just about the same time as Reg was going to bed.

"Ugh. I can't get up that early."

"This isn't just curiosity about who manufactures those truffles," Corvin pointed out grimly. "This is life and death."

And Reg knew from the circles under his eyes and their conversations that he had not been sleeping well since he became aware of the cluster of deaths in the magical community.

"I have to get *some* sleep," she told him.

"If you have cleared your calendar, then head to bed early so you can get a little in," he said sensibly. As if it were perfectly reasonable to suggest that Reg could just go to sleep at will.

At Reg's look, he offered, "I could make you a sleeping potion if you like. It will have you off to the sandman in no time."

"Yeah? Is that what you've been using to stay as fresh as a daisy?"

Corvin flushed a little, redness creeping up his throat. "Someone who has been using such potions for many years may find himself becoming immune to its effects. It takes much more to put me to sleep now than when I was a young man."

Reg nodded knowingly. "Oh, I see. It's just because you're so old now."

He chuckled. "Don't get fresh with me, youngster."

Reg wasn't going to take any potion that Corvin offered her. But if she was going to have to get up early in the morning, she'd better get home and at least try to nap.

CHAPTER TWENTY-THREE

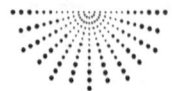

*T*hings did not go well.

And, truth be told, Reg hadn't expected them to.

Forcing herself to go to sleep early was not something she'd ever been able to do. She didn't know how shift workers managed it, though she'd talked to several of them and they all thought it was a skill that anyone could learn.

But many foster homes had tried to train her to sleep at a reasonable hour, and it had never worked.

By telling herself that she was just taking a nap to refresh herself, she managed to get half an hour of dozing in, still aware of everything around her and every noise the cottage or Starlight made. Unused to Reg sleeping during the evening, Starlight did not understand why she was in bed and kept wandering in to check on her, meowing and nosing at her in concern.

One half-hour, disturbed nap was insufficient to prepare her for another full day. At some point, she was going to crash. Probably right at the most inconvenient moment.

She had a tall travel mug of strong coffee with her as she climbed into Corvin's car. He looked at it.

"Is that as full of sugar as the ones you order at The Witches' Brew?"

"No. Just enough…"

He shook his head. "Ruins the coffee."

"You drink it your way; I'll drink it mine."

He nodded and shifted the car into drive. He said nothing as they drove the short distance to the Gingerbread Lane Bakery. Reg was thinking about what he had said the day before about myths of his kind luring children into the forest. Julian had said something similar to her when they had discussed people living in remote locations in the woods.

They both got out of the car as soon as Corvin stopped. No pausing to decide on a strategy. They both felt the urgency of figuring out where the truffles had come from, who was making them, and their agenda.

And, of course, how to stop them.

Bringing the toxic nature of the truffles—if that really was what had killed three people—to light was only the first step. They needed to ensure that whoever had made and distributed them was stopped.

Reg couldn't believe how early they had to be there to talk to the owner of the bakery when it opened. She never got up that early. And she knew from Erin that the baker would have had to be there a couple of hours earlier to get product into the ovens so that the freshly baked bread and muffins would be ready when they opened their doors.

An employee turned on the Open sign and unlocked the door as they approached it. She was startled at having someone waiting right outside the door on opening, but stepped back out of the way and smiled a greeting.

"Good morning! Welcome to Gingerbread Lane. We hope it makes all of your baking fantasies come true."

That might be laying it on a little thick. But Reg smiled as though she were charmed. "What a nice little place. I can't believe I've never been here since I've lived in Black Sands. I've always just grabbed my baking at the grocery store. But you're right," she turned her head to address her comment to Corvin, "this place is great. Look at the variety? And I could just swim in the smells…"

The employee who had opened the door smiled in approval and took her place behind the counter with another woman, this one older, probably the proprietor or head baker.

Reg stepped up to the display case and looked closely at the various baked goods on offer. Even though she never ate first thing in the morning, her stomach grumbled at the delicious sights and smells.

"This is amazing," she enthused. "And I'm not even a breakfast person."

"What are you in the mood for today? Are you looking for something specific? Or do you want me to just let you browse?"

"Maybe... one of those big, gooey cinnamon rolls..."

The baker laughed and nodded. "Those are very popular!"

Corvin walked around the bakery, looking at the display case, the mural on the wall, and the price board above the employees' heads. He stopped at the cash register.

"You have these too. The Magical Bites."

"Mystical Morsels," the younger employee, whose name badge said Amanda, corrected. "They're really good. We give out free samples, but almost everybody has tasted them by now and just comes in to buy more bags."

"I heard they're delicious," Reg said as the baker selected a roll, put it into a box, and slathered it with icing. She was nearly drooling on the floor, watching and anticipating how it would taste.

"You have more of the Magical Morsels in stock, then?" Corvin asked.

"Mystical Morsels. There are several different varieties. Do you know which one you want?"

"I don't know." Corvin glanced at Reg. They would have to check with the victims' families about that. Had they selected a particular variety? Was only one kind of morsel tainted? "Just the original, I think," Corvin guessed. "I assume that's what you sell the most of?"

"Yes. Although I really like the Enchanted Energy to help get me moving in the morning."

Corvin made a noise of acknowledgment. "Could I see a bag of the original flavor?"

"Of course." Amanda agreed. She opened a cupboard and looked through it, choosing one of the paper bags like Sarah had given Reg.

She displayed it to Corvin, but pulled back slightly when he reached for it. "They are fourteen ninety-five."

"I have allergies," Corvin said irritably. "I need to look at the ingredients before I know if they are safe."

"Oh, I see. Of course." Amanda placed the bag on the counter so Corvin could pick it up and look at the label more closely.

Reg paid for her cinnamon bun while he perused the package. "How does it look?" she murmured to Corvin.

"Nothing obvious." He raised his voice to address Amanda. "Where did you say these are made? They are local?"

"Oh, no." Amanda shook her head. "We bring them in. They're from a bakery in…" Amanda looked at the other woman. "In South Carolina?"

"In Tennessee," the woman corrected.

"Oh, Tennessee," Amanda nodded. "I knew it was one of those."

"Tennessee," Reg repeated, disturbed by the connection. Erin's bakery was in Tennessee. But of course they were not related. Not everyone in Tennessee knew each other. Erin wasn't the only baker in the state. And she wasn't a chocolatier or confectioner. Of course, anyone could make truffles.

Corvin looked at her questioningly, but Reg shook her head and didn't try to explain why the creator of the truffles being in Tennessee had surprised her.

"Are you going to buy those, then?" Amanda asked.

Corvin looked at the bag of truffles in his hands, taking a moment to make his decision. Reg could sense his thoughts as he considered the matter. Maybe he was deliberately sharing them with her to help him decide. It would be good to have a bag of the truffles to examine more closely for a spell or contaminant, or maybe even give some to Marta for the drug lab to investigate. And they would have the details of the distributor or manufacturer in the fine print of the label. Maybe even other evidence, like fingerprints, though Reg didn't know if that would matter.

But taking a possibly cursed object into the car and home with them might not be the best idea. Did they need to eat the truffles for them to take effect? Or did they have a curse that would begin to affect them as soon as they paid for them and took them out of the store? Or they could even be working on Corvin now, tempting him to buy them and take them home with him.

"They look good," Reg told him. "I think you should get them. If they're safe for you, that is."

Which was a waffle answer, because who knew whether they were safe for him to possess? But she had told him to get them.

If they were safe.

Corvin rolled his eyes at her, irritated. "Yes," he finally told Amanda. "I'll get them. Do you... know the bakery that makes them personally? Or the person who makes them?"

Amanda glanced over at her boss. The older woman frowned at Corvin. "Why do you want to know that? Why do you care who makes them?"

"I'm sure you know about the farm-to-table movement. People like to know exactly where their food comes from and how it is sourced," Corvin pointed out. "It's perfectly valid to want to know where your food comes from."

"Well, I don't know about that," she grumbled. "But no, I don't know them personally. I took a phone call from the distributor who wanted to know if we would display them as directed and sell them for a percentage of sales." She shrugged. "Diversification is the name of the game, right? I might not make them myself, but the customers like them and I get a little back on them."

Reg imagined she probably made a good amount back on them. Stores all over town would not be stocking the truffles if they weren't making a good return. It had to be profitable.

Amanda rang up the truffles, Corvin paid for them, and they left together.

CHAPTER TWENTY-FOUR

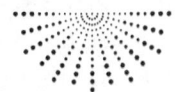

Sitting in the car, Corvin looked at the cinnamon roll in Reg's lap.

"Was that your cover story?" he asked dryly.

"Absolutely," Reg agreed, grinning. "You don't think I eat like this all the time, do you?" She stabbed the roll with her plastic fork and tore a bite away from it. She put it in her mouth and moaned in pleasure. "Forget truffles! These are the best."

"Maybe we're wrong. Maybe it is the cinnamon rolls that are doctored," Corvin suggested. He turned the key in the ignition and pulled out onto the street.

Reg froze with her fork over the cinnamon roll.

Any of the people that they had talked about could just as easily have gone to the bakery and purchased a cinnamon roll. There was nothing to say that they had all only bought truffles. Helen had spoken of sweet and salty treats before bed, not truffles in particular. There were cookies and other commercially baked goods in Chelsea's kitchen. She could have had a cinnamon bun too. The Shoop family had clearly had other sweet treats around as well. And, of course, Sarah and Marta had easy access to the bakery, just like anyone in the neighborhood. It was within walking distance of Sarah's house.

"We need to ask them what the victims had to eat in the few days before their deaths. Whether they all had truffles or something else from the bakery. Or... something the same from the grocery store. We're only guessing that they all had the truffles in common."

Corvin nodded. Reg stared down at the cinnamon roll on her lap, wondering what to do with it.

"You already had a bite," Corvin said. "If it is enchanted, it's too late for you. You might as well finish it."

Well, he was the expert. She didn't know very much about cursed objects. If it was poisoned, then eating more of the poison would make her sicker, but if there was enough poison in one cinnamon roll to kill a person, then they should have had more than three deaths. And it should have been pretty obvious that the poison had come from the cinnamon rolls. The others had been sick, showing possible symptoms for "a few days," which suggested poisoning over a period of time, not just one cinnamon roll.

She should be safe to finish eating it. And the smell was intoxicating. Was that how the truffle-eaters felt about the Mystical Morsels? More than one person had said that they were addictive.

"Do you think they're actually addictive?" Reg asked aloud.

Corvin looked at her. "Cinnamon rolls?"

"No, the truffles. Everyone says how good they are, how addictive. Do you think they really are?"

"I doubt it." Corvin rubbed his whiskered chin and shook his head. "People say a lot of things. When they're talking about food and say that it is addictive, they aren't really talking about an addiction like coke or heroin."

"But what if they are? Maybe the paleness and irritability are withdrawal. And the other personality changes... those could be signs of addiction. Dulling the senses. Tamping down emotions."

"Well... I suppose that's a possibility. I wouldn't have thought of it, but... I couldn't say you're wrong. But do you really think they're laced with something like an opiate?"

"Can you take it that way? And they're not destroyed by the baking process?"

"Truffles aren't baked."

"So it could be? Do you think Marta would have them tested if we told her they might have an illegal drug baked—mixed in?"

"Not unless the victims had some indication that they had died from an overdose. I assume they know the signs of overdose or would run a routine tox screen in the case of an unexplained death. In Patty Meiers, at least."

"Yeah, if they thought she died of an overdose, they would have to test for that to prove it. And if one or more of them tested positive for a drug, then could we take the truffles to Marta and convince her to have them tested?"

"I'm not sure I could convince her. Maybe you could. We have to establish that each of the victims ate the truffles, first and foremost. And that they didn't all eat something else, like bread or cinnamon buns from the bakery. Or something that they bought at the grocery store or a fast-food joint... It's not as easy as it seems."

Reg groaned. "I just want to figure it out and get them to test the truffles so that we can prevent more deaths."

"We'll figure it out," Corvin assured her. "Let's talk to each of the interviewees again. It won't take long to do if all we have to do is find out whether the deceased had eaten Mystical Morsels."

Reg took a deep breath in and released it. "Okay. Let's do that." She took a couple more bites of the cinnamon bun. They were just as good as that first bite. She felt like she could keep eating the bakery's cinnamon buns all day long.

"We should go to talk to Chelsea first. She's not that far from here."

"That's where I'm going."

"Oh." Reg laughed at herself. "I guess you knew that."

"I did," Corvin agreed.

Reg watched out the window and continued eating her cinnamon roll. She was just finishing it and licking off her sticky fingers when they rolled up in front of Chelsea's townhouse again. Reg gazed at the blank, sightless windows of the house.

"Do you think she's home? Maybe we should have called first."

"We're here. May as well give it a try."

It was earlier in the day than the last time they had visited, and there were no children in the street, which Reg found both reassuring—at least they were not being stalked by pixies—and unsettling. The neighborhood was too quiet. She supposed the majority of the residents were still at work or school.

It seemed eerily quiet. Several birds wheeled and called in the sky overhead, their voices sounding mournful and lonely.

Corvin knocked on the door. They waited for a few minutes. Corvin knocked louder and pressed the bell several times, even though they could not hear it ringing inside the house.

Eventually, the door opened a crack, and a mussy-haired Chelsea stood there in a ratty bathrobe looking at them, squinting in the sunshine the door allowed through.

"Who are you, and what are you doing here? You want me to call the cops?"

"We were here yesterday, Chelsea," Reg told her, moving closer to the door to peer in at Chelsea. "Corvin Hunter and Reg Rawlins? We were talking to you about Patty?"

"What are you doing here again and why are you here so early? Why are you even up already?"

A girl after Reg's own heart. Reg wished that she wasn't awake. The cinnamon roll and coffee had given her a good energy boost for a while, but she knew she would end up crashing, and crashing hard.

"We just had one more question for you. I'm sorry it's so early."

Corvin snorted. Reg glared at him, telling him in her mind to keep quiet and look remorseful instead of condescending. Corvin looked away and, when he looked back, his face was appropriately shamefaced.

"What question?" Chelsea demanded. "I answered all of your questions yesterday. You don't need anything else from me. Seriously."

"Just one question—whether Patty had eaten any of those Mystical Morsels."

Chelsea's brow furrowed. "The chocolate truffles? Yeah, sure she had. So did I. What difference does that make?"

"We think…" Reg looked at Corvin for his help with an explanation, but he didn't say anything, letting her take the lead. "We think they might have had something to do with her death. If you still have any around… you should probably not eat them."

"Death by chocolate?" Chelsea gave a bark of laughter. "Give me a break. I told you it was her favorite food, but that doesn't mean that was what killed her. I don't think you *can* eat enough chocolate to kill yourself."

"We think they might be… tainted."

"Are you serious? But I ate them too, and I'm fine."

"Maybe you didn't have as much as she did? Or maybe you are more resistant to the… poison or pathogen or whatever it is."

"Well, like I said, the girl did love her chocolate. She definitely had more than I did. If I wanted any, I had to make sure that I took a few from the bag and hid them away for later." Chelsea rubbed her eyes. Reg wasn't sure whether it was out of tiredness or emotion. She still wasn't feeling any strong emotions from Chelsea. Mostly just annoyance. She was tired. She didn't want to deal with company, and she certainly wasn't going to invite them in.

"We'll go," Reg reassured her. "Just… I don't think you should eat any more of the truffles if you have any left."

"Yeah? They're poisoned and you think I probably shouldn't be eating them?" Chelsea asked sarcastically.

"Well…" Reg shrugged in embarrassment. "I just don't want anyone else to get hurt."

Chelsea nodded. "Well, I'm not going to eat any more of them, so you can put your minds at rest."

"Good. Thanks."

The other woman studied Reg for a minute, then shook her head as if she couldn't understand what they were doing there. She shut the door. They heard her bolt and chain it.

Reg turned to Corvin. "One down, two to go."

After Corvin buckled his seatbelt, he pulled out his phone and tapped a number.

"Who is that?" Reg asked.

"After getting Chelsea out of bed... I think we'd better give Helen a heads-up, just in case."

Reg nodded. "Good plan."

Corvin waited with the phone against his ear, frowning. There was apparently no answer, and he reached voicemail. He left a brief message and hung up.

"I guess we go see the Shoops next."

"You're not going to call them first?" Reg asked as he pulled away from the curb.

"Do you really think that with three children in the house they will still be asleep?"

"Well... no, I guess not. But they might be at work."

"I'll take my chances on at least one of them being home. Even with the lack of emotion we saw yesterday... I don't think they'll both be back at work right away. People will expect them to take a little more time off to grieve."

Reg shrugged at this. She supposed he was probably right. She couldn't predict what people would do when they were addicted to truffles and their emotions were suppressed. Maybe they would go back to work, and maybe they would just want to sit at home and stare at the TV all day, whether it was turned on or not.

CHAPTER TWENTY-FIVE

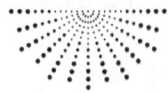

*T*hey met with a replay of the previous day with Minnie the dog barking and scratching at the door, threatening to eat the intruders if they did not retreat immediately.

Again, she was whisked away to another room where she was locked away to keep her from interrupting the visitors.

Andy Shoop looked at Corvin and Reg and scratched the back of his neck, frowning. "I wasn't expecting to see you back again," he said. "I hope this isn't going to become a habit. We need the time to mourn."

"I know," Reg agreed. "I'm so sorry. We wouldn't disturb you again if we didn't think it was really important. Some new information has come to light, and we needed to warn you..."

Andy glanced aside at Corvin, waiting for him to back Reg up. It wasn't the first time a man had ignored her and looked to the man in her company, expecting him to be in charge and to confirm that what she said was true or valid. Gary probably didn't even realize he had done it, but it ranked just the same.

Corvin just nodded. "Maybe we could come in. This will only take a minute, but you may want to sit down..."

"Is it that bad?" Gary demanded. "How could it be any worse than what we have already been through?"

Reg and Corvin stood there, waiting for him to invite them in. Eventually, Gary nodded and motioned for them to enter.

They took the same seats that they had the previous day. Gary in his dad chair and Suzie slightly behind him. Reg looked around. Different toys were on the floor, testifying that the children had been home between the two visits, but all was quiet now. Even the youngest children must be in school or early childhood education.

"Mr. Shoop… we noticed when we were here last that you like chocolate truffles," Reg introduced the topic gently. "Were they that new brand? Mystical Morsels?"

"You came for my truffles?" Gary laughed.

"No… we didn't come for them. But we wondered whether Andy had eaten any in the days before he died."

"Of course. We all had some. I told the kids that they could only have one per day but, of course, they didn't all follow that rule. Those truffles disappear pretty darn fast. Andy was a mischievous little guy and got into a lot of things. And he was gluten-free, so he got a few extra truffles, because he couldn't have the cookies that the other kids got."

Reg swallowed, her throat suddenly dry. She wished that the Shoops had offered her a glass of water. "He was gluten intolerant?"

"He has celiac disease," Suzie explained. "If he has gluten, it will make him sick. It could even be life-threatening when he—" She cut herself off from what was clearly a well-worn explanation. But Andy no longer had any future in which the gluten might cause him more severe health problems.

"I'm sorry," Reg apologized. "I'm so sorry. We didn't come here to make things worse for you. It's just that… we think that it's a possibility that the truffles could be… the thing that has caused the recent deaths in the magical community."

"You think the truffles killed Andy?" Gary demanded, sounding angry.

He was probably defensive. He felt guilty at the idea and lashed out.

"We think they might be," Reg agreed, trying to make her

response as unemotional as possible. She had already apologized for the pain they had brought him. If she appeared too vulnerable, he would just attack where he saw weakness. "We're still looking into it."

"You're looking into it. You're not the police. Just what do you think you're going to accomplish?"

"If we can get enough information—we hope to be able to convince the police that there is something going on and put a stop to it!"

He considered that and didn't argue.

"You think the other children are in danger?" Suzie asked. "Should I take them to the hospital?"

"I don't even know what to say to look for. We don't know whether it is poison, or magic, or what. I don't know if it affects everybody, or just some people. Or even if all of the truffles are an issue, or just a few of them. But everyone who has died has been eating them."

"Everybody in town has been eating them," Gary pointed out. "They're all over the place." He scowled and shook his head. "How could someone do that? You think it's intentional? I mean, they've blanketed Black Sands with these things, and they're tainted? Is this some kind of terrorist thing? Someone with a grudge? Someone who is just out to kill people?"

"We don't know that it's intentional," Corvin said. "We've barely narrowed down the possibility that it is the truffles. Maybe it is a mistake. An accident or oversight. Or third-party tampering. We don't know that it is actually the manufacturer who is responsible."

"Well, you'd better find out. Whoever is responsible should be going to prison! They killed my son!"

Even though Reg could feel his anger breaking through, the emotion was still dampened, not nearly as strong as she expected. Likewise, the grief was held at a distance. After a few days, she didn't think it was still shock and disbelief. There was definitely something wonky going on with his emotions.

"We're doing our best to find out," Corvin agreed.

"They need to pay for what they have done."

"I'll throw out the rest of the truffles," Suzie said, sounding disappointed. "It's too bad… they were really good."

"Do you still have some of the same bag Andy had eaten from?" Reg asked. "It would be good if we could have that particular batch tested. In case it's just a certain batch or a few bad truffles."

"I don't know…" Suzie looked at her husband as if asking him about the reasonableness of this request.

"We can't throw them out or give them to *them*," Gary objected, nodding toward Reg and Corvin as if they were not there. "We'll just finish the last few and won't buy anymore."

"You can't eat more of them!" Reg was stunned that he would even suggest this. "You could be poisoning yourself. You have to stop eating them now."

"Well, we could get another bag. It's probably just that one bag that is a problem. We could give you what's left of that bag and get a fresh one…"

"We don't know how many of them are contaminated. You can't be eating any more of them."

"But…"

"It sounds like you're addicted to them," Corvin said. "You're talking about eating something that could end your life, just because you like them. What kind of sense does that make?"

"Well, I doubt if they're *all* dangerous. Someone has just tainted a few of them. There have only been three deaths, and this town must have consumed hundreds of truffles in the last week or two. Thousands of them. Not everybody who eats them dies."

Reg looked at Suzie, hoping to appeal to her good sense. "If you could just go get that bag, so that we know it is out of here and can get it tested. And then…" Reg shook her head, glancing over at Gary and back again. "You *can't* get any more until this is resolved."

"Do you *really* need that bag?"

Reg and Corvin nodded.

Suzie sighed. She got up from her seat and went into the kitchen. They heard a cupboard open and close. Reg strained her ears for the rustling of the paper bag, indicating that she was taking a few out before giving the rest of the bag to Reg. She didn't *think* Suzie had taken any out, but she couldn't be sure.

Suzie handed the bag over very reluctantly. Reg was keeping an eye on Gary, who looked like he was ready to jump out of his dad chair and take the rest of the bag. She could imagine him grabbing the bag from her and shaking what remained of the truffles directly into his mouth and down his throat before she could prevent him. And then what? Going into convulsions and dying on the floor in front of them? Or would he go on as if everything was perfectly normal and then die in his sleep? Or would he be completely unaffected? There was no guarantee that the remainder of the truffles were tainted or that Gary would react to them. Maybe the dosage wasn't high enough or he was immune to its fatal effects, with it affecting his emotions just enough to be noticeable.

Gary caught her eyes on him and settled back into his easy chair, sinking into it and closing his eyes for a moment as if to school himself to stay there. "Take them," he said. "Just take them now and get out of here."

Reg looked at Corvin and rose to her feet. She didn't want to stay there any longer than necessary. She didn't want to take the chance that Gary would lose control and come after the truffles before she had gotten out of the house.

"Thank you," she told Suzie, aware that her voice sounded tentative and uncertain instead of confident. She needed to get out of that place before she lost all ability to make an independent decision.

She and Corvin left together, Reg clutching the bag as tightly as possible between her finger and thumb. They didn't follow her or make any warnings or threats. Reg knew that Gary was doing his best to tamp down the addictive impulse to go after the truffles. Hopefully, once they were out of the house, his desire would decrease, and he and Suzie wouldn't go out and buy more.

"Well, good work," Corvin told her as they returned to the car.

"You're right; that bag of truffles might be important evidence. You need to make sure you keep track of it so that you can testify as to what happened to it between the time you took it from Suzie Shoop and the time you handed it over to the police."

"Testify? Like in court?"

"You know that the police need to be able to prove chain of evidence. You would need to state that it was in your possession. Since they weren't the ones to take it from the house."

"I'm not going to court."

Corvin sighed and rolled his eyes. He started the car. "Does it look the same as the other bag? No differences?"

"I think so." Reg picked up the bag of truffles they bought at the bakery. She held them side by side and turned them both around at the same time so that she could compare all sides. "Yeah, it looks like it. I don't see any differences."

"Does it have a lot number or expiry date?"

Reg looked closely for a stamp of some sort. There didn't seem to be one. "No, I don't see anything like that." Reg tried to read all the fine print on the back of the bag. She was not a reader, and the tiny type was difficult to sort out.

Tennessee. Why would a company in Tennessee be blanketing a small town in Florida with Mystical Morsels? The name of the manufacturer was listed as ABC Industries. The letters swam. No, not ABC Industries, but ACB Industries. She blinked and tried to keep the letters from swapping around again. Yes, definitely ACB Industries.

Auntie Clem's Bakery?

There was no way that it was Erin's bakery. She baked. She didn't make truffles. Though Reg knew she had branched out into ice creams and frozen treats for sale during the summer. Why not truffles, if they were a good seller? Especially if they were naturally gluten-free.

"I still can't get her," Corvin said.

Reg looked at him. "What?"

"Helen. No answer. Just keeps going to voicemail."

"Oh. Well, why don't we go by there anyway? We still need to talk to her. If she isn't home… she isn't home. We can go on to the police station and give Marta these truffles. I don't want to hold on to them any longer than necessary."

CHAPTER TWENTY-SIX

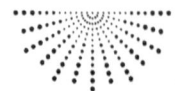

*W*hen they pulled up to Helen Papadakis's house, they saw a police car and several people standing outside the house talking and looking toward it. As Corvin pulled over to the curb a few doors down so that they wouldn't be in the way, an ambulance whooped once. It stopped in front of the house next to the police car, both nose-in toward the curb with their back ends out into the driving lane.

The paramedics who climbed out of the ambulance were not moving quickly.

"Oh, no," Reg murmured.

Corvin didn't say anything, his eyes intent on the scene, taking everything in.

"She didn't answer the phone," Reg said.

He nodded.

The paramedics took a long time to get a gurney out of the ambulance and wheel it up to the house.

Of course, the police officers in attendance might have already evaluated the patient and informed the dispatcher that she would need to be transported to the hospital but, in Reg's experience, the paramedics went in to treat first, and then retrieved the gurney once the patient was stabilized.

Or when there was nothing to be done.

Reg rubbed her abdomen, trying to quiet her tense muscles and writhing gut. "Tell me I'm wrong."

Corvin shook his head. "No. I don't think you're wrong." He sighed. "Let's see what we can find out."

They got out of the car and joined the people on the sidewalk.

"Is Helen okay?" Reg asked the nearest woman. "Did something happen? Is she sick?"

"Did you know Helen?" the woman studied her carefully. "I don't remember you ever being with her."

"We were just there yesterday, talking to her about Beverley. I can't believe it…"

"They haven't said anything definite yet," the neighbor said. "But I don't think the news is good."

"Her family found her?"

"She missed our morning walk. Didn't check in. Didn't answer the door or the phone when I called her. The others must all be at work, but I don't have their numbers. I have a key. So I called them for a welfare check and gave it to them. I was afraid… well…"

"She didn't think it would be long after her sister died," Reg said. "But I didn't think it would be this quick."

"There, now." The woman patted Reg's arm reassuringly. "She's in a better place and she and Beverley are together again. They could never be happy apart."

"I know, but…" She looked at Corvin. "If we'd gotten here sooner…?"

"There's no way to know." He looked significantly at the friendly neighbor and jerked his head for Reg to separate herself so they could talk. They wandered down the sidewalk away from her, looking at the house as if it might tell them the story. "As far as we can tell, it takes a few days for the poisoning to take effect, so it was probably too late for us to do anything for Beverley. She was already sick."

"But they're *all* already sick, from what we could tell. They're all acting irritable, stoned by whatever is in those truffles. Does that mean we're going to lose the rest too? More members of the Shoop family? Sarah? Marta?"

"Don't jump to conclusions. I don't think it is fatal to everyone who eats them. Maybe only those who eat a lot of them or have a genetic predisposition. Or they're already sick in some way. Or they need to eat a certain amount. We've only had three deaths."

"Only three in the magical community. Four now."

Corvin frowned and shook his head.

"You don't know if there have been any in the non-practitioners," Reg pointed out. "You only thought it was strange that three people who should have had much longer lives had passed away suddenly, so close together. But did you ask yourself—or anyone— how many non-practitioners died during that time? Of natural causes?"

He stared at her. "You're saying that it could be higher."

"A lot higher!"

"Hmm." He didn't say anything, thinking about the possibility. But Reg knew she was right. They had no idea how many people had died in Black Sands since the truffles had arrived on the scene, nor how that compared with the usual numbers. If they all appeared to be natural deaths, the police wouldn't have any reason to be suspicious. They would just keep funneling those cases through to the medical examiner's office and think nothing of it. Unless there were a *lot* more deaths or several people in the same household died at once. Which apparently had not happened yet.

A uniformed police officer came out of the house. He made his way toward the neighbor and his car. Reg and Corvin wheeled around to intercept him.

CHAPTER TWENTY-SEVEN

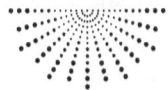

*I*s it true?" Corvin asked, closing in on the policeman. "Is Helen dead?"

The neighbor looked irritated that Corvin would insert himself into what should have been a conversation between her, as the person who had made the call to the police, and the officer who had come to fill her in on what had happened. The cop frowned at Corvin and looked him up and down. "And who are you?"

"We were talking to her yesterday. We might have even been the last ones to see her alive."

Reg felt sick at the idea. She knew that Corvin was only using it as an excuse to muscle in on the investigation, but it could be true. They might have been the last ones to ever see Helen Papadakis alive.

"When did you see her?" The cop asked, deciding he'd better see what Corvin and Reg had to say. "How did she seem at the time?"

"She was pale. She seemed... distant. Like something was wrong."

"I understand she had just lost her twin sister."

"Yes. But she certainly wasn't expected to die this soon. She

119

hadn't been sick. Her doctor gave her a clean bill of health," Corvin invented.

"Even doctors don't always know. Where grief is concerned…"

"She didn't seem to be grieving that deeply," Corvin said.

"Of course she was," the neighbor said indignantly.

"She said it wouldn't be long before she saw her sister again. It sounded like she had given up. Maybe she had made a plan. Does it look like poisoning? Had she eaten or drunk anything? Were there pills or anything else on the bedside table?"

He was assuming she had died in bed. She might not have. She could have been anywhere. It could have been a fall or something violent. It could have been in the bathroom.

But Reg assumed not, since the cop acted like it was a natural death. He wouldn't be acting that way if she had obviously done herself harm. He would be calling in detectives and the medical examiner's office. There would be people there to collect forensic clues. As it was, it looked like the lone law enforcement officer was the only one who was going to show up at the scene.

The cop shook his head. "No, I didn't see any pills or a note. I don't think it was suicide."

"But she could have eaten something. A few hours before bed."

"Well… yes. Of course. But what reason do you have to think that she ate something poisonous? What did she say to you yesterday?"

"Just that she didn't think she would be here that much longer."

"Well, that was true."

Corvin huffed. He wasn't getting very far with the cop. "So, as far as you can tell, she just died in her sleep?"

The cop shrugged. "It really isn't up to me to give you any of that information. I was going to give the woman who called us a brief report, but what standing do you have in this case? As far as I can tell, it has nothing to do with you. You're just some bystander trying to get details on something you know nothing about."

Reg felt a wave of heat from Corvin, but knew it was not directed at her. Corvin smiled at the cop and slid a little closer to him, leaning forward. It wasn't quite the same as when he was seducing a woman, acting flirty and giving compliments, exuding the rose-scented pheromones that would cloud her brain. Instead, he looked interested and attentive.

The effect was the same. The policeman's expression softened and he got a little dopey looking. His cheeks turned pink.

"I can assure you that I do have an interest in the case," Corvin said. "I was interested in the case long before you were called. If you will just confirm that Helen died the same as the others, appearing to just pass in her sleep…"

The cop made an effort to arouse his mental faculties. "What others?"

Reg could smell the scent of roses. Corvin was really laying it on thick, hoping to get all of the information he would need from this man.

"Her twin sister. A girl that died at a club. And a little boy who apparently had nothing wrong with him, and yet… never woke up."

"I don't know anything about any other cases. You're saying they are related?"

"Undoubtedly. That's why I asked about the truffles."

"Truffles?" the cop echoed, dazed.

"Had she been eating the truffles? The same ones that poisoned her sister?"

"Poisoned truffles?"

"The brand name is Mystical Morsels. I'm sure you would find some either in her kitchen or whatever she had been eating before going to bed last night. You need to locate those truffles. It will be important to keep the chain of custody clear. They need to be sent to the medical examiner's office with the body to be properly tested."

"I didn't see any truffles."

"Oh." Corvin raised his brows. "Then I guess you had better go look. Because they were definitely here yesterday. If you've tampered with the crime scene or been sloppy in this case, you are in such a world of trouble…"

"I'll take another look." The cop set his jaw and forced himself to withdraw from them and return to the house. Corvin smirked at Reg. "You just have to know how to talk to these people."

The neighbor was still looking offended.

Corvin tried to smooth it over. "You've been such a help," he told her. "A good neighbor to Helen all of these years. I know she appreciated your help and attention."

"Helen was a delight. It was never a burden to check in on her or to help her with anything. She and Beverley were such lovely, warm people."

"Just like you. Kindred spirits."

The neighbor blushed profusely, turning a pretty shade of pink. "No…"

"She spoke of you often, told me how much you did for her. She surely appreciated your company and those morning walks…"

"Well, I did too. It wasn't just for her. I got so much out of them. I'm really going to miss her. Both of them. We were like the three musketeers."

"You were. She said so often."

The neighbor kept looking at Corvin, trying to get a good look at him without staring. She had to know that Corvin was not a relative or someone who had visited her friend regularly. On the other hand, Reg didn't actually know how well he had known Beverley or Helen. They had been familiar to him when he saw the obituary. Maybe she was judging him too harshly in assuming that he had never been friends with either woman.

It wasn't long before the cop was out of the house, holding up a paper bag of truffles and looking satisfied with himself.

"They were just behind something else," he told Corvin. "That's why I didn't see them the first time."

"Ah, good. So you'll send those along with the body for proper testing."

"Of course. You don't need to tell me my job."

Corvin smothered a laugh. "No, of course not. I didn't mean to imply that you don't know what you're doing."

The cop returned to his squad car to get a proper evidence bag.

Corvin looked at Reg. "I think we can go now. Unless you want to see her when they bring her out."

"No, no. I don't need to see her."

"If she spoke to you about what she knew…" Corvin talked to Reg out of the side of his mouth, as if to keep his words a secret from the neighbor, who shouldn't have been eavesdropping.

Reg shook her head. She wasn't going to try to raise Helen's spirit out in the open for everyone to see. That would be morbid and would upset more people than just the friendly neighbor. She nodded toward the car so they could continue the conversation privately.

"You're sure you don't want to talk to her spirit?" Corvin asked. "Her presence is probably still pretty strong around a body that new."

"No. I don't want to talk to her here in front of everyone. If we need to, I can try to raise her later, at home, when it is quiet and I'm in the right frame of mind."

Corvin nodded. "Okay. Good to know."

They each got settled in the car, and Reg looked around. "Now what?" she asked. "This was a bust."

"We got confirmation that they had eaten the truffles."

"Well… yeah, I guess."

"We didn't know that before. We thought we were on the right track, but we didn't know for sure that they had all eaten the Mystical Morsels."

Reg supposed that they had come a long way in a few hours, going from a wild theory to at least being able to settle some of the details.

But she still felt guilty about not having reached Helen any sooner. Could they have saved her if they had put more effort into it? If Reg had started a day earlier, when Corvin had wanted to? If she had started in the morning instead of waiting until the evening? If they'd had just a few hours more of a head start on the case, could they have saved Helen?

CHAPTER TWENTY-EIGHT

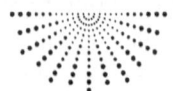

*W*hat are you thinking about?" Corvin asked. He probably had a pretty good idea, since she could never completely hide her thoughts from him.

Reg indicated the bag that she had taken from the Shoop house. "I'm wondering where these came from."

He nodded. "We'll have to see if we can find out who owns the company, where they are based. See if we can talk to someone."

"I might know."

"You do?"

"Might."

"How do you know this? You must be getting quite a hit off of that bag."

"It says ACB Industries in Tennessee."

"Yes."

"My foster sister lives in Tennessee. And runs a bakery called Auntie Clem's Bakery."

"ACB."

"Yeah."

"Well… maybe it's time to give her a call."

"I'm not sure this is something I can ask her on the phone."

Reg had called Erin a number of times since she had moved to

Black Sands, but she always got the feeling that Erin thought she had gone off the deep end. Granted, there were things that Reg couldn't talk to her about. There was no way she would believe any of the *more unusual* aspects of Reg's life or the things she had discovered about herself. But Reg still wanted to talk to her. It was hard to keep all of that stuff from creeping over in the course of a conversation, so Erin probably thought Reg was on her way to the loony bin.

Corvin raised an eyebrow. "Then what do you want to do?"

"I was thinking… maybe I should go see her face to face."

"A road trip?"

"Well… that would take a lot of extra time."

A smile tugged at the corner of Corvin's mouth. "Oh, I see. You want to travel eight hundred miles to see this foster sister of yours, but you don't want to drive. Or fly, I assume."

"That's right," Reg agreed. Although flying wouldn't be bad, if she could do it on her own rather than in an airplane. Still, it would be too far to fly to Tennessee under her own wing power. It would be much faster by other methods.

Corvin glanced around. "Do you want to pull over somewhere or go home first?"

Reg didn't want to take Corvin to her house. He might be behaving himself throughout the operation, but she still couldn't trust him not to try to overcome her if they were alone in the cottage.

"Just from here. Anywhere you think it is safe to leave the car for an hour or two."

In a few minutes, Corvin pulled into the parking lot of a park, positioning the car under the shade of a couple of trees, protected as much as possible from the Florida sun. No one would notice it parked there for a few hours. People visited the park to walk, play, or picnic and spent several hours there. No one would think the car had been there for an excessive length of time. Not unless the trip took a lot longer than Reg expected.

"Okay." Corvin looked at her. "I'm coming with you."

Reg nodded. She had fully expected that. He was the one who

had first identified that the cluster of deaths might be suspicious and was invested in finding out what was going on.

Corvin smiled and held his hands out toward her. Reg didn't need to do more than to touch his arm to take him along with her, but she took both of his hands in hers anyway. An electric shock ran through her that took her breath away. But it was not unpleasant, and after a second or two, settled into a vibrating buzz rather than anything painful. Reg blew out her breath.

"That was intense."

Corvin said nothing. Reg closed her eyes and imagined Erin in Bald Eagle Falls. It had been over a year since she had seen Erin. Things had been a little uncomfortable; Erin never had believed in Reg's powers, even when she had seen them with her own eyes. Reg pictured the bakery to start with but, if she appeared there without warning, who knew how many old ladies would have heart attacks. So she thought instead of Erin's house, the pretty little one that used to belong to her aunt Clementine. It must be nice to inherit a house and a storefront like Erin had. It had been a lucky break for her, just the thing to help her break out of poverty and get on her feet.

But Reg hadn't ended off too badly either. The legacy she had been left by her family *was* a little more unusual.

She could smell the freshly cut grass of a neighbor's lawn, feel the sun on her face, and hear the birds in the trees. When she opened her eyes again, she was there. Standing in the yard with Corvin, holding hands. She let go of him and looked around.

"You're getting very good at that," Corvin told her.

There had been a few rough trips before Reg had gotten the hang of sending herself from one location to another. It was much easier if it was a place she had been to before. Sending herself to unfamiliar places could be disconcerting. Or dangerous.

Corvin looked around. "This is her house?"

"Yeah. What time is it?"

Corvin looked at his watch. "Nearly noon."

"She'll still be at the bakery for a few hours. But she might be able to take some time off over lunch."

"Do you know the way?"

"Uh… I don't remember exactly. We'll start out, and if I get turned around, we can ask someone. Or use the GPS on my phone."

"Sounds like a plan. Lead the way."

The house and the bakery were closer together than Reg had remembered. They found it pretty quickly. Nice and convenient for Erin. She could easily walk between the two if she didn't want to take her car. A little exercise to keep her trim.

CHAPTER TWENTY-NINE

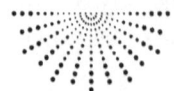

he bells over the door rang as Reg walked into the bakery followed by Corvin. There was a blond girl at the counter whose eyes flicked over to Reg. She smiled a greeting and spoke past the customers who were in line in front of Reg.

"Welcome to Auntie Clem's Bakery. Have you been here before?"

Reg struggled to remember the girl's name. They had met the last time Reg had been in Bald Eagle Falls, but Reg really hadn't paid her much attention. She was Erin's assistant.

And her best friend. And tenant too, if Reg remembered right. It was hard to keep it all straight. She honestly hadn't been listening to anything about Vic.

That was it, Vic!

"It's Vic, isn't it?" Reg asked. At Vic's blank look, Reg prompted her memory further. "My name is Reg. Reg Rawlins."

"Oh!" Recognition flooded Vic's features. She nodded vigorously. "I'm sorry, I should have recognized you. It's not like everyone walks in here dressed like... that."

Reg twirled her brightly colored skirt and straightened the scarf around her head. She *hoped* that not too many looked like that. It was part of her trademark. Her brand. Reg was a psychic; she wanted the world to know it just by looking at her.

"Is Erin in?" Reg asked.

"Yes, of course." Vic turned around and called into the kitchen. "Someone here to see you, Erin."

The other customers who were there ahead of Reg were all looking at her, trying to figure out who she was or expecting her to do something interesting. Reg considered speaking in tongues just to see how they would respond to an act but decided against it. She was there for something serious. She needed to be serious instead of showing off like a kid just because she was in Erin's hometown.

A slim, petite baker with dark hair sticking out from under her baker's hat came through the doorway from the kitchen to the front counter and looked around. She saw Reg and her eyes went wide.

"Reg! What are you doing here? I can't believe it!" She opened the hinged portion of the front counter to enter the customer area and gathered Reg in a hug. "How are you? Did you just get into town?"

"Yeah, I did. I'm not planning to be here for very long, but I wondered if we could talk somewhere privately for a few minutes."

"Uh… well, we're right in the middle of the lunch rush right now. Could you wait a little while until it slows down? I'll have another employee coming in this afternoon, and I can take some slack time."

Reg looked around. There were chairs and tiny cafe tables at the front of the store, so she and Corvin could sit down for a while and discuss matters until Erin was ready to see them.

"Sure. We could just wait here until you are ready."

"Great." Erin looked back at the bakery display case. "Can I get you something for lunch while you're waiting? A muffin? Energy bar? Dessert? The pizza pretzels are great for lunches; I can warm one in the microwave for you."

"Pizza pretzels sound great," Corvin said. "Let's do that."

Erin's eyes went to Corvin for the first time.

"Oh. I'm sorry, I didn't even realize you were together. I'm Erin Price." She offered her hand to Corvin.

He sensed Reg's warning not to touch her sister, and instead of taking it, just gave a little bow.

"Pleased to meet you. I'm Corvin Hunter. I'm sure Reg has told you all about me."

Erin looked over at Reg for guidance as to what to say. Reg shook her head. "Why would I tell her all about you? You're not anybody."

Corvin chuckled. "Well. You might have at least mentioned me."

"If I did, it would just be to warn her to stay away from *anyone* with the last name of Hunter."

Erin gave an uncertain laugh, confused by Reg's response. "Well, it's very nice to meet you. I'll throw some pretzels in the microwave for you, and then we can catch up after the lunch rush is over."

Reg nodded. It hadn't been that long since she had finished her cinnamon bun, but she could manage a pizza pretzel or two. She motioned to the chairs, and she and Corvin took a couple of seats. They waited for the pretzels, looking out the window and at the customers in the bakery in turn. A lot of curious glances were being thrown in their direction.

Reg wondered how many townspeople would remember her from the last time she had been there. There had been some suspicion toward Reg because of her psychic gig and a certain amount of jewelry might have gone with her when she had left Bald Eagle Falls, though that really wasn't her fault. Erin had been kind enough not to mention it. Hopefully, no one whose jewelry had disappeared would find out Reg was there while she was visiting with Erin. Reg didn't fancy a trip to the local jail with Erin's partner, Officer Handsome. Or Terry or whatever his real name was. She didn't quite know how Erin had landed that one.

She did her best to block any negative thoughts circulating around the bakery. She couldn't control everyone, and could only dampen the negative thoughts and suspicions toward her, not eliminate them completely, but maybe that would be enough.

Erin returned from the kitchen with a couple of plates, with two pretzels on each, and made her way through the waiting customers to Reg's table, smiling and making comments to the customers who were waiting, making them feel like they were noticed and it would not be long before they were served. She was good at that. Erin always had been a people-pleaser and much better at the social stuff than Reg.

"Enjoy," she told Reg and Corvin with a smile. "I'll be with you as soon as I can."

Reg knew she should say, "Take your time," but she didn't want Erin to take her time. Reg had transported there because they urgently needed answers, not because she wanted a sentimental reunion with Erin. Instead, she just nodded, and she and Corvin took the first bites of their pretzels.

"Oh, these are great," Corvin groaned. "They really hit the spot." He had probably been up for hours longer than Reg and he hadn't eaten anything from the Gingerbread Lane bakery. After a few more bites, he shook his head. "I thought you said that she was your foster sister."

"She is," Reg agreed, confused by his comment.

"Then where did she get the magic she needed to make these?"

Reg rolled her eyes. "I don't think making gluten-free baking takes a magical gift."

Corvin's eyes widened. "These are gluten-free?"

"Everything in the store is. Did I not mention that?"

"No." Corvin looked over at the display case. "Everything? Are you sure? Maybe she just has gluten-free alternatives."

"No. Everything here is gluten-free. Including that pretzel."

"That's unbelievable. I've never tasted a gluten-free bread with this kind of flavor and texture. I would never have guessed."

"She's a good baker. Great to live with someone who loves experimenting with baked goods!" Reg smacked her lips. "And if you tell her something is just a little off, she'll make a whole new batch to address that issue."

Corvin laughed. "Sneaky, Regina. I'm shocked."

"I was doing her a favor. Helping her to hone her craft. If I hadn't been there to challenge her and get her to produce the most perfect gluten-free baking, the bakery would have failed."

"Well, yes, I'm sure it would have," Corvin agreed. "You are a selfless sister. An inspiration to us all."

Reg grinned and had another bite of pizza pretzel. It was good that she'd given Erin such a hard time about her baking when they were kids. It had turned out very well.

They munched in companionable silence for a few minutes.

"Did you notice something?" Corvin asked.

Reg looked at him. She looked around the bakery to see if something had happened that she should have taken notice of, then back at him again. "What?"

"There are no truffles on display."

Reg looked closely at the bakery display case and the counters flanking the cash register. Corvin was right. There were no truffles in evidence. Her stomach muscles loosened and her shoulders relaxed slightly.

"I didn't realize how tense I was," Reg said, massaging her shoulders and neck. She blew out her breath in a long, controlled stream. "ACB Industries can't be Erin. If she was making those truffles, she would have some here."

Corvin nodded his agreement. "Even if she was set on poisoning everyone in Black Sands, I am sure she would still sell untainted truffles here. Why go to all of that work to make truffles and not sell any in your own store?"

Reg nodded her agreement. Looking into the display case once more, her gaze was pulled to a platter of chocolate chocolate chip brownies. She remembered Erin's moist, gooey chocolate chocolate chip brownies. If she warmed them in the microwave so that the chips melted, it would be like eating them straight out of the oven when Erin baked a new batch.

Corvin chuckled. Reg tore her eyes away from the brownies and looked at him.

"I can hear you mooning over those brownies from here," Corvin laughed.

Reg's cheeks warmed. "You haven't had her brownies."

"No, but apparently, they are very good."

"They are."

"And you're sure she's not a witch? Sometimes minor witches don't even realize they have powers…"

"She's not a witch," Reg insisted. "Erin is about as buttoned-up normal, boring, and earthbound as you can get. She's got lots of experience and a real knack for making gluten-free baking, but it's just hard work and practice."

"And talent," Corvin added.

"And talent," Reg agreed, "but *not* magic."

CHAPTER THIRTY

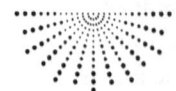

The crowd of waiting customers thinned out. Erin wiped her shiny forehead with the back of her wrist and smiled at Reg when she came to the table.

"Well, things should be quiet now until the after-school/pre-dinner crowd. And Bella will be in for that." She looked around. "Do you want to talk here or go for a walk? Or somewhere else? If you need something else to eat…"

"No," Reg shook her head. "This will hold me. Though… I'm going to need some dessert to take home with me."

Erin laughed. "Of course." She turned to look back at the display case. "Are you eyeing the brownies?"

Corvin flashed Reg another look that said, "See, what did I tell you?"

But it wasn't a psychic insight on Erin's part, just experience.

"Of course," Reg agreed.

"I'll package some up for you. Do you want to talk here?"

"No. Somewhere more private… if that's okay."

"Sure. Where are you parked? We could go over to the house."

"Actually, I'm parked close to house, so that would be great."

"Okay. Let me get you some brownies and then we can go back to the house for tea or lemonade."

* * *

They drove back to the house in Erin's yellow bug. It was a bit cramped for Corvin's long legs, but he preferred riding a couple of blocks in a cramped car to walking back in the heat. Erin let them into the house and disarmed the burglar alarm. They were immediately accosted by an orange cat with a raucous meow. Reg remembered him from the last time, though he had grown since then.

"This is Orange Blossom," she told Corvin. "Erin rescued him as a kitten."

Corvin did not like cats, but he tried to look interested and reached down to pet Orange Blossom when the cat rubbed up against his leg, yowling noisily.

Blossom instantly whirled and hissed, swiping at Corvin with unsheathed claws. Corvin jerked back, but not quickly enough. Blood welled up from several nasty scratches across the back of his hand.

"Oh, Blossom!" Erin yelped. She grabbed at the cat. "I'm so sorry, Corvin. I've never seen him act like that before. I'll put him in the bedroom and then I'll grab the first aid kit."

It took her a minute of wrangling before she was able to grab the angry cat and take him to one of the bedrooms. He continued to meow loudly on the other side of the closed door.

"I can't believe how loud he is!" Reg laughed.

Erin shook her head and went into the bathroom to get first aid for Corvin's hand.

Reg motioned to Corvin. "Let me see that."

He held his hand out to her, palm down, and Reg held her own hand an inch above it, sending heat down into the wounds.

"Don't heal it completely," Corvin warned, "or your sister will have some questions."

Reg stifled a giggle. It wouldn't be the first time Erin had questions about Reg doing something impossible. Erin had eventually ceased to notice or to ask about what she had seen. It was safer that way. If she bought into Reg's "delusions," she could be the next one sent to the funny farm.

Erin returned with antiseptic and bandages. She took Corvin's hand and wiped off the blood. She leaned close to examine the shallow scratches.

"Oh, those aren't as bad as I thought they were. I'm glad! I've never seen him behave like that before. Do you have a cat or dog at home?"

Corvin shook his head. His lips were pressed tightly closed. Reg would have thought that he was in pain if she had not already mostly healed his scratches.

"No. I don't like animals."

"Oh." Erin looked up from her work on Corvin's hand to his face, obviously disappointed by this information. "That's too bad."

"Animals don't seem to like me."

Erin and Reg exchanged looks. As cat owners, they both understood that animals were good judges of character. Starlight had always responded violently toward Corvin, just as Orange Blossom had. They knew he was a predator, not a harmless caretaker like most humans, and they did not like him. They wanted to protect their humans from any potential harm from the threat they sensed.

Reg gave a little shrug to show that she understood and was aware of the problem with her companion, and she and Erin did not say anything about it out loud. They didn't need to. Erin might not have actual psychic abilities, but she was intuitive, and she and Reg had enough shared experiences that Erin could read her.

"Okay, I think that should do," Erin said, giving Corvin's bandaged hand a pat. "I really am sorry about that. I should have asked you if you were okay with animals before you came in."

Although it was polite and apologetic, Reg heard Erin's words as a rebuke. Corvin should have told her that he didn't like animals when Orange Blossom had first come in and not have attempted to pet him.

"Let's have some tea. Or did you want lemonade?"

"Tea is good," Reg agreed. She looked at Corvin and he did not object.

They followed Erin into the kitchen and sat down when she motioned to the table.

"Can I help you with anything?" Reg asked, knowing that the answer would be no.

"All I need to do is boil the kettle. Everything else is all ready."

That wasn't entirely true, as Erin still had to bus the tea tray to the table and get out teacups and spoons for them. But there wasn't a lot to do. She pulled some cookies from the freezer and thawed them in the microwave without asking.

It wasn't like Reg was going to object.

She might have to go on a diet when she got home but, while she was in Bald Eagle Falls, she was going to take every opportunity to sample Erin's baking.

CHAPTER THIRTY-ONE

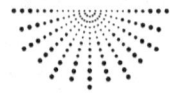

S o…" Erin finally sat down at the table with them. "Not that I am not happy to see you, but what brings you here? What was it you wanted to talk about?"

"Have you ever heard of ACB Industries?" Reg asked.

"ACB Industries." Erin frowned. She considered the question for a minute and then shook her head. "No, I don't think I ever have. You thought that I might have because it is ACB? Like Auntie Clem's Bakery?"

Reg nodded. "Yeah. I was kind of surprised when I heard of ACB Industries in Tennessee and wondered if there was a connection."

"*Industries* is sort of a… well, a name I would associate with things like oil drilling or building heavy machinery. What is it they do? Do you know, or is that part of the question?"

"The one thing that we know they do is make truffles."

"Chocolate truffles?"

"Yes. They're all over town in Bla—in Florida. They just showed up in the last couple of weeks, and they're suddenly being displayed and distributed everywhere. The package says that they are manufactured by ACB Industries, which is based in Tennessee."

"Huh. Well, I can tell you for sure that it isn't me. Truffles would be a nice product to add for Christmas or special gift boxes. Hang on a sec…"

Erin got up and walked out of the room. Corvin raised a brow at Reg.

"You think she's telling the truth?"

"Yes. Erin really doesn't lie. If she does, she gets really uncomfortable, and I can tell. And like you said, if she made truffles, there would be some at Auntie Clem's. It doesn't make sense that she would make them and ship them all off to Florida."

Corvin nodded his agreement. Erin returned a moment later with a small planner binder. Reg watched with amusement as Erin opened it up and made a few notes under a section toward the back.

"Does this mean that you're no longer using random receipts and the backs of envelopes?"

Erin's cheeks reddened. She closed the binder and ran her fingers affectionately over the cover.

"Yes, I've broken that habit," she agreed. "I love my planner and use it for everything. I don't go anywhere without it." She hesitated momentarily and then opened it to give Reg a peek. "I have everything organized in here. My schedule for the next few months, my task lists to keep everything under control at Auntie Clem's, ideas for new products, everyone's phone numbers… before, I would write random notes down on whatever was handy and they would all be crumpled up in my purse and pockets. But now, even if they're just random thoughts, they are all recorded and organized in here." She patted the pages, smiling.

"Why not put them on your computer or phone?" Corvin suggested. "What happens if you lose your planner? If you have it electronically, you have a backup."

Erin bit her lip and gave a little grimace. "I know. But I've barely converted to a binder. Catch me in another year or two and maybe I'll be able to make the shift to electronic."

"You can still print stuff out and put it in your binder," Reg suggested.

Like Reg was an expert on planning systems. She didn't even

use reminders on her phone. She had an appointment book on her kitchen island that Sarah wrote appointments into. Reg hadn't purchased it and rarely wrote anything in it herself. She had to remember to write down any new appointments so Sarah wouldn't double-book her. Reg was certainly no shining example of using a modern scheduling system. She should be using one of those programs that told people what time slots she had open and they could book them automatically online. And Sarah could log in from the house to add other appointments without making the trek across the yard to the guest cottage to check Reg's schedule and write it in.

"Someday," Erin said with a shrug.

Reg nodded. "Yeah. Me too. Someday."

"So, do you know anything else about this ACB Industries?" Erin asked. "We could look it up online."

"Uh… yeah, that would be a good idea. I didn't think about that."

"You just thought that you would drive all the way to Tennessee to ask me, without doing an online search first?" Erin shook her head. "I assume you were on your way somewhere else and just decided to stop in here for a visit."

"Yeah," Reg agreed. Of course she wouldn't have made the trip if she'd had to drive all that way. She would have just phoned Erin. But she didn't immediately come up with an excuse as to what they were doing in Tennessee. If she made up some public event, Erin could look it up online and see that it didn't really exist. Reg could say that she was visiting a friend, but then she would have to come up with a name and why she had to see that friend. She was tired and didn't feel the need to come up with a believable lie if Erin didn't ask for further explanation.

"Let's see…" Erin pulled out her phone and tapped through a few pages and then performed a search. Reg could have done the same on her phone. Only she was usually distracted by videos, ads, or strange rabbit holes. "ACB Holdings, an accounting firm, a cannabis company," she shook her head, "air conditioners. I don't see any ACB Industries…"

Reg shrugged. "Well, it was a long shot. I didn't actually expect to find anything out, but..."

"Oh, don't give up yet! There's another way to use the phone to get information!" Erin tapped again and put the phone to her ear, grinning at Reg.

Reg smiled and shook her head. That was one of Erin's talents. She always knew who to talk to about what. She had friends everywhere. People liked and trusted her automatically.

"Terry," Erin said, greeting Officer Handsome on the phone. Reg couldn't help turning her gaze toward the front door to make sure he wasn't about to walk in on them. She knew he would need evidence to arrest her for something, but who knew what he had managed to find out about her since she had been there last? He might have discovered outstanding warrants, aliases, or more information about the personal items that had disappeared around the same time as Reg had.

After reassuring herself that he wasn't about to burst in on them, Reg turned her attention back to Erin, who was trying to talk Terry into looking up information on ACB Industries for Erin.

"They apparently make truffles," she was telling Terry. "I don't know what else they might make, whether they are into cookies or other baked goods. I wouldn't want people to confuse them with Auntie Clem's..."

Terry was apparently not in a cooperative mood.

"I know," Erin agreed. "But it would be nice to know, just to make sure that we're not competing and confusing people..."

She listened for a bit, shaking her head and rolling her eyes a little at Reg. When she eventually terminated the call, her shoulders slumped. "Sorry, I thought he might be able to give me something."

"It's okay," Reg said. "Don't worry about it."

"You know who might be able to help..." Erin flipped open her planner and went to her telephone directory pages. She turned the pages for a minute and then apparently found the one she wanted. She looked at the time on the clock on the wall before tapping the number into her phone.

Reg exchanged a look with Corvin, wondering who Erin was calling this time. Another cop? Her friend Vic?

"Josh," Erin greeted. "How are you doing?" She waited, listening to what he had to say. "Hey, I was wondering if you could help out a friend of mine. She's trying to find something out about a company called ACB Industries. But I can't find them online, so I don't know... anything about them other than that they distribute truffles."

She paused again and listened.

"No, the chocolate kind. I know you did really well in tracking down that construction company, when all you knew about them was their logo. So I thought this would be a piece of cake for you."

Another pause. Erin's eyes wandered around the kitchen. She took another sip of her tea. Her eyes strayed to the cookie still left on the plate. Clearly, she had a dilemma. She was trying to watch what she ate, but there was a cookie right in front of her that no one else was eating... she couldn't just throw it out. She couldn't freeze it again...

"I'm at home. Yes, ACB Industries of Tennessee is all I know. And that they make truffles. Okay. Thanks."

She hung up and smiled at Reg.

"A private investigator?" Reg guessed.

"Investigative journalist."

"Ah." Reg swallowed. She wasn't sure she was comfortable with this. "I don't want him reporting on this..."

"Reporting on what?" Erin shrugged. "I just asked him to look into who owned that company."

"But won't he want to know why? If he looks into it and something leaks out..."

"That's not going to happen," Erin assured her. "I know Josh. If you're worried about him saying something to someone, I'll make sure he knows not to. To keep it confidential between us."

"That's not the way investigative journalists work," Corvin said.

"Well, you don't know Josh. He won't if I ask him not to."

They were all silent for a moment. Reg sighed.

"How long will it take him, do you think?"

"I don't know. Hopefully just a couple of hours. He's a pretty good researcher, even on stuff that can't be found online. Did you have something else you wanted to do for a couple of hours? If you need to go, I can just call you with whatever he finds. But you sounded like it was something you needed to know."

"Yeah… we'll stick around here," Reg agreed. "Maybe… go for a walk in the woods. This land is all yours, right?" Reg gestured to the woods out the back, beyond the fence.

"Yes, that's right. Until you reach a fence line or road. You want to go for a walk?" Erin cocked her head, looking bemused. "I never thought you enjoyed walking in nature."

"Well… people can change. Mature. Tastes change."

"And you have a handsome man to walk with you," Erin teased. "Do you like long walks in the woods, Corvin?"

He put his hand on his chest, smiling. "You got me there, Erin."

Erin nodded knowingly.

"I'll just call you when I hear from Josh then. Is that what you would like?"

"Yeah, that sounds good," Reg agreed.

CHAPTER THIRTY-TWO

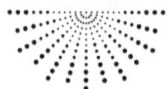

*R*eg stood up, and Corvin followed her lead. "I'll see you in a bit, then," Reg told Erin.

After they walked through the backyard to the woods and were out of sight of the house, Corvin turned his gaze to Reg.

"She's right about you not being one for long walks in the woods," he pointed out. "So why the subterfuge?"

"What?"

"Why are we out here?"

"Well, I didn't want to be in Erin's way. I'm sure she has a lot of things she wants to do. She's okay, and she's not involved in this thing, whatever it is. That was what I was worried about. And I figured… we don't actually have to wait here. We can just go back home and wait for her call."

"You don't want to say goodbye to her?"

"I don't know. I could come back to say goodbye."

But they kept walking deeper into the forest and didn't take the jump back home. Reg was reluctant to go home, where all they would find was more bad news. More people dying. No leads on where the truffles had come from or if they were really the vehicle for the poison. Neither of them was really eager to leave.

Reg had never noticed the difference between the forest in Tennessee and the wild areas in Florida. It was much drier, with less moss, and there were different kinds of trees. Maples and conifers instead of mangroves and cypress. The ground wasn't marshy. It was a nice change of pace. Though, as Erin and Corvin had pointed out, it wasn't like Reg spent a lot of time walking through the woods at home.

A crow cawed nearby, and Corvin looked around for it, a slight smile on his face. It was true he didn't like cats and dogs, but he was more in tune with birds, especially crows. Corvids, Sarah had told Reg. Corvin's namesake.

Reg looked around nervously. She hadn't thought, before coming out, about who she might run into in the woods. She had just thought about giving Erin her space.

"What is it?" Corvin asked, frowning down at her. "Who is here?"

"Uh. No one. Yet. Maybe we should go back into town. Do some window shopping along Main Street. They have a cute little General Store, and there's a bookstore next to the bakery you might like."

"You want to go to a bookstore?" His tone was skeptical.

"No, I thought you might like to, though."

Corvin raised one eyebrow, waiting for her to explain why she was suddenly nervous about remaining in the woods.

Reg cleared her throat and didn't tell him. "Come on. Let's go back to Main Street."

"Or we could go home."

"No, I decided I'm not ready to go back yet. Not when they won't be any further in the investigation than when we left. And if I go and come back, that will take extra energy. I decided I want to conserve it for just one jump."

"I could always give you more energy."

Reg felt a wave of warmth that left her with goosebumps when it dissipated. She gave a little shiver. "No, I don't need any more if I am just careful with how I expend it."

He shrugged, smiling as though she were missing out on something good. Reg turned around and they started to retrace their route into the woods.

"This is private property!"

Reg and Corvin froze at the voice that snapped out at them from behind. Reg felt Corvin gather his strength. She put her hand on his arm to stop him. Even through his cloak, she felt a buzz of electricity.

"Don't," Reg warned. "It's okay."

They turned slowly. Reg held her hands at shoulder height. Corvin followed suit, his mouth curling up in amusement. It wasn't as though he couldn't face any attacker who tried to get the drop on them. And he and Reg together were a pretty potent combination.

As Reg had expected, a tall woman with hair as red as Reg's stood back in the trees, a shotgun cradled across her arm, looking them over. A crow fluttered down and perched on her shoulder. It took a moment before the light of recognition came into the game-keeper's eyes.

"I remember you. I can't remember the name... is it Reg?"

Reg nodded. "Yeah, Reg Rawlins. Erin's sister."

Adele nodded slowly. "That's right. Foster sister. There's *obviously* no blood shared between you two."

"So what?" Reg challenged. "That means we're not sisters?"

Adele shook her head. "Just making an observation." Her eyes turned to Corvin. "You, I haven't seen in these parts before."

Corvin took a couple of steps toward her, casual, lowering his hands and reaching one out as if offering to shake. Adele took a step back, her lips tightening. She raised the gun slightly.

"That's far enough, stranger. I don't like people approaching me without an invitation."

Corvin studied Adele, interested. He definitely wanted to get closer to discover more about her powers and see if she were a likely target. Reg sent him warning signals. He did not want to mess with Adele.

Corvin was amused. He was stronger than any other practitioners they knew. And that probably included Reg herself.

Becoming the leader of his coven had built up his powers, maybe making it easier for him to access and utilize what he had taken from the Witch Doctor.

"My name is Corvin Hunter," Corvin introduced himself smoothly to Adele. He smiled, and exuded warmth and the smell of roses. "I'm pleased to meet you, Miss…"

"Missus Windsor," Adele cut him off, appearing unaffected by his charms. "But you can call me Adele. I don't stand on ceremony here."

"Adele, it's a pleasure." He shuffled his feet forward, getting infinitesimally closer to her. "Another redhead. A member of your extended family, Reg?"

"There is no relationship between us as far as I know."

But Reg had wondered about the old lore of witches having red hair and had wondered whether she and Adele were both descended from the same line at some point. Many generations ago, on one of Reg's human lines.

"What are you doing back here?" Adele asked Reg. "I warned you the last time you were here about tampering with powers you didn't understand. And now…" She shook her head and didn't finish.

And now here Reg was, with full knowledge of the powers that had been unknown to her before, and at least an inkling of how to use them and the rules surrounding them. She no longer stood before Adele as just a con artist who had learned to cold-read people by their facial expressions and body language. But now, as a true psychic and firecaster, with a mix of siren and other blood running through her veins. She was a very different person from who she had been the last time they had met.

"I needed to see Erin and make sure she wasn't mixed up in a situation we're having back in—back at home," Reg told her. "I didn't come to cause any trouble or step on anyone's toes."

"You are different. You are brighter. More… aware."

Reg nodded. "I have met some people who have… opened my eyes."

Adele nodded and looked back at Corvin, her mouth pursed

like she'd been sucking on a lemon. "But you still don't understand the powers you play with."

"Am I supposed to figure everything out in a year or two?" Reg gestured toward Corvin. "Some of you guys have had hundreds of years to learn it all."

Adele's eyes narrowed at Corvin. "I don't like your kind in my woods. You need to leave."

CHAPTER THIRTY-THREE

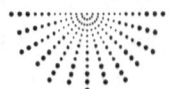

*H*e's with me," Reg said. "When we're done, I'll take him home."

"You shouldn't have brought him here."

"No. Maybe not."

"I'm the leader of one of the oldest, most prestigious covens in America," Corvin told Adele, steel in his voice even as he smiled pleasantly at her. "I really don't see how you can object to that kind of person going for a walk in the woods. They aren't really *your* woods, are they?"

"I'm tasked with keeping them safe."

"Even Erin Price doesn't really *own* them, does she? How does a person own a part of Mother Earth?" Corvin challenged.

"I bow to the traditions of the nation we live in. But no, of course, no one owns Nature herself."

"You see? We all believe in the same thing. There is no reason for you to be exclusionary. I have as much right to walk through these woods as you do. As free people."

"Your kind and mine do not mix. I believe in freedom and nonviolence, but I will defend myself and the people I have sworn to protect. The sheep have to be guarded from the wolves."

It wasn't the first time Reg had heard Corvin called a wolf. She supposed that all the axioms about wolves in sheep's clothing applied.

"We won't be here long," she told Adele. "There are people at home who need us. People who are dying, and more will die if we don't get the answers we came for."

Adele blinked, her eyes widening in surprise. "Who is dying? What kind of answers do you need?"

"It isn't anything to do with you. Unless you happen to know something about the ownership of ACB Industries."

"ACB?" Adele repeated. "Auntie Clem's Bakery?"

"As it turns out, no. But I had to make sure. Erin has asked her friend Josh to investigate who might be behind ACB. We really need to know. We need to find out who is killing people in Bla—at home."

"I know you are in Black Sands," Adele said. "You don't need to keep that from me."

Reg had hoped not to reveal where she was living to anyone in Bald Eagle Falls. But apparently, Adele already knew that. Maybe unsurprising; she probably had a network of witchy friends all across the country and had heard at some point of the new psychic making waves and causing trouble in Black Sands. Maybe she had heard about some of the entities and creatures Reg had faced there. Was Adele impressed?

If she was, she didn't show it. She didn't want Reg in her woods, near her boss, or in Bald Eagle Falls. Adele would happily send her on her way if she could.

"We need to find this information," Reg reiterated. "Once we have it, we will leave."

"What is going on in Black Sands?"

"People are being poisoned. By some truffles, we think. The packaging refers to ACB Industries in Tennessee, and I had to ensure Erin wasn't mixed up in it somehow. But she says she has no idea who it is."

"Why haven't I heard anything about this?"

"Why would you?" Corvin challenged. "Is there some reason people would report to you what was happening in Black Sands?

It's a little out of your territory, isn't it? A bit farther than you would want to walk on your ramblings."

"I have friends. I like to know what's going on in the world, especially as it affects others of my faith."

"Then cooperate with us instead of trying to block us. All we want is to rest and regenerate in nature. Isn't that what these woods are here for? We have Erin's permission to be on her land."

Adele jerked her head and shoulder in a movement that was half a nod of acknowledgment, half a shrug. She lowered the gun so that it was no longer cradled in a ready position, but pointed at the ground.

"An' ye harm none," she cautioned.

Reg and Corvin both nodded at the oft-quoted law. Adele started to turn away from them.

"The bird," Corvin said, stopping Adele. "Is he your familiar?"

Adele turned her head slightly to look at the bird perched on her shoulder. "Or am I his?" she asked obliquely. "Skye is a free creature. He may spend his time as he chooses."

"Would he guide me?"

Reg blinked at Corvin, surprised by the request.

"Guide you where?" Adele asked.

Corvin shrugged, pressing his lips together in a thin smile. "Where he will."

Adele looked at Skye again. Reg strained her faculties to hear the communication that passed between them, but was not able to catch it. Birds were on a different wavelength than cats. Reg could usually sense the mood or purposes of Starlight and other cats, but birds were alien to her. Her brain did not connect to theirs as easily.

Skye launched himself from Adele's shoulder and landed in a branch above Reg and Corvin. He let out a loud, rough caw. When Reg looked back at Adele, she was gone, vanished into the trees. Skye called again and flew out of the tree he had perched in, going deeper into the woods.

Corvin nudged Reg. "let's go."

"Where are we going?"

"We're following the bird."

She shook her head. "Following it where?"

"We will know when we get there."

"That's crazy. We're going to follow a crow deep into the woods? How do you know it isn't going to lead you to a ginger-bread house where a little old lady is waiting to cook us and eat us?"

"If one of my kind was in these woods, I would know. What are you afraid of? We're not going to go far. And now that Adele has given us permission to walk the woods, you don't need to fake an interest in going to a bookstore."

Reg laughed, sheepish. "She's kind of weird. It freaked me out a bit when I was here before and she told me not to play with powers that I didn't know anything about. That was... before."

"Before you decided to play with them," Corvin offered with a wolfish grin.

"Yes. Exactly."

He chuckled. "Follow the bird."

They made their way through the woods, keeping a close eye on the black crow leading them. Reg was not quiet, crashing through the brush. Even if she tried to tiptoe and walk as silently as Corvin, she seemed to step on every dry twig and loose rock.

"I thought that 'as the crow flies' meant a straight line," Reg complained as they turned to follow Skye in a new direction.

"What a crow *can* do and what he chooses to do are two very different things."

"What do you think you're going to find? Some treasure? Some... mysterious answer? What?"

"Nothing."

Reg shook her head. "Nothing?"

He smiled again. "Follow the crow."

It was hot and, even though they were shaded by the trees and there was a light wind, Reg was hot and sweating and was sure they had been traipsing back and forth across the little wooded area for at least an hour.

Eventually, Skye stopped and didn't seem inclined to fly any farther. He sat above them on a branch and just croaked and murmured under his breath.

"I've never heard a bird make that sound before," Reg said.

Corvin led her over to a log and made a show of brushing it off for her to sit down. Reg let out a deep sigh and sat on the edge of the log. She looked around at the beautiful glade; dappled sunlight shone through the leaves and branches overhead. It felt like they were on a different planet, just she and Corvin. There were no sounds of the city around them. No screens. No insistent voices. Just distant birds chirping and the rustling of branches and leaves fluttering overhead.

"This is it?" Reg asked.

Corvin nodded.

"Nothing," Reg repeated. "There's nothing here."

He touched her lip. "Then say nothing. Just *be here* for a moment."

Reg opened her mouth to speak, but he tapped her lip again, reproving her.

Reg sighed again and closed her mouth. She folded her hands in her lap, closed her eyes, and acted like she was sitting in church services as a child. It hadn't mattered to anyone whether she got anything out of the sermons and lessons. Only that she sat quietly and still. Two of the hardest things for her to do.

Corvin sat on the log beside her.

It was both comfortable and uncomfortable for her to sit with him. She was glad to be off her feet and take a break from wandering the woods. And to be away from any demands or reminders of what was happening in Black Sands.

It was even comfortable sitting next to Corvin, feeling his warm body and his presence so close to her, yet without his trying to charm and ensorcel her.

At the same time, she wanted to move around. To scratch an itch. To check her phone and her social networks. To call Marta Jessup and see where they were on the mysterious deaths and whether they had decided to call them murder. And she knew that Corvin could turn on his charms at any time and try to charm her by stealth, gradually increasing his pheromones and other charms before she noticed.

Reg's phone rang.

Skye cawed loudly and flew away. Reg opened her eyes and looked around.

Nothing had changed, but she could no longer sit there waiting for nothing. She jumped to her feet and pulled out her phone.

"Erin?"

CHAPTER THIRTY-FOUR

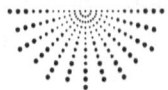

*R*eg was quiet while they hiked back to Erin's house. She had to trust Corvin's sense of direction. She had gotten too turned around following Skye back and forth or in circles around the woods. If she were back in Black Sands, she probably could have figured out her location by sensing the proximity and direction of the ocean. But she didn't know Bald Eagle Falls well and had no idea where the falls were. She hadn't ever seen them.

Corvin didn't have much to say. Reg didn't know whether he was lost in thought about the deaths in Black Sands or had deep thoughts about something else. Had he been affected by their encounter with Adele or something to do with Skye? She'd never known him to want to go off and meditate before. But then, he wouldn't exactly tell her that, would he? If he wanted to be alone, he wouldn't seek her out to tell her.

She was sweating heavily when they broke through the edge of the woods and she saw the back of Erin's house. She hadn't noticed before that there was a window nestled high up under the peak of the roof. Erin must have an attic room that Reg hadn't previously been aware of. Did she hide away up there? Have secrets she didn't disclose to anyone? Erin had always been a private person, not sharing her thoughts with everyone else. The two of them had shared some bits and pieces of their pasts and their dreams. Still, as much as they had wanted to be sisters taking on the world together, their world views and their plans for the future had just been too divergent for them to have any hope of success. They'd had to go their separate ways.

Did Terry know Erin's secrets? Had she found a soulmate in him, or was he just a safe relationship? Erin had dealt with some nasty people in the past, and Reg was sure that Terry must seem like a hero by comparison. Was Erin starstruck, comfortable, or really in love with him?

Reg paused before stepping up onto the porch, for long enough that Corvin turned and looked at her, waiting for her to join him.

"Everything okay?"

"Just a little out of breath. We covered the return trip pretty quickly."

"Yeah. Sorry about that. I didn't think about my longer legs."

She waved a hand at him. "It's okay. Just need a minute to catch my breath." Reg wiped her forehead. She didn't want to walk back into Erin's house dripping with sweat. That was just gross. She pulled off her head scarf, blotted her forehead and face, and tied it back on again. She swept her red box braids back over her shoulders and took a deep breath. "Okay. Let's do this, then."

* * *

"Oh, there she is," Erin said, when she heard the door open and Reg and Corvin entered the house. She stepped into the doorway between the kitchen and the living room to look at Reg. "Hi. I hope I didn't cut your walk short."

"No, we're good," Reg assured her.

"Why don't you sit down? I'll bring out some lemonade."

Reg had to admit that cold lemonade sounded heavenly just about then. She sighed and she and Corvin walked into Erin's living room.

The person that Erin had been talking to was just a boy. An older teen or young adult, still in the final stages of gawkiness before he would fill out his slim frame, bright and eager eyes, a preppy haircut. He looked at Reg and Corvin with interest. They made a good pair. Reg was used to getting stares from the normal folks in Black Sands and other places she went. The headscarf and brightly colored skirts and blouses attracted attention. Like they were intended to. And she was sure that most of the men in Bald Eagle Falls did not walk around in a black cloak, especially in the warm Tennessee sun.

"Uh, hi," Reg greeted. She reached out her hand to shake the boy's.

"Hi. I'm Joshua Campbell," he told her, taking her hand in a confident grip.

"Nice to meet you, Joshua."

She felt a well of sadness around the boy. He smiled and presented himself as a confident, clean-cut kid, but she was willing to bet he had a tragic past. Holding on to his hand, she turned it over and examined his palm. He didn't pull it away. Reg examined the lines on his hand, but was more interested in the feelings she was getting from him. There was a lot of pain in his past. And if she was right—and she was sure she was—he had been captured and held against his will at some point. This young pup! He should have been at home enjoying his life. School, basketball, friendships and, instead, he had been dying. Starving to death while his mother searched for him.

But he was strong and had risen back up, even in the wake of that terrifying event. He was now back in school, stronger than before, willing to take on the world no matter what dangers it held.

Reg slowly released his hand. "I hope your future will be happier than your past."

Joshua snorted. "Me too."

Erin returned with the lemonade. She smiled at them and set a tray of filled glasses and a pitcher on the coffee table. "Everyone help yourself. You're so flushed, Reg."

"We wanted to get back. Might have hurried a bit too fast."

Reg helped herself to a glass of cold lemonade and drained half of it before coming up for air. "That hits the spot," she gasped.

Erin looked amused. "Why don't you have a seat. You met Josh?"

Reg looked back at the boy, the information gradually connecting in her brain. "This is your investigative reporter?"

"Don't judge a book by its cover," Erin warned. "He's had several articles in our newspaper and he's very good at what he does."

Reg nodded. She believed it. He was smart and strong, both physically and mentally. But did he have the connections to find out the information she needed?

She sat down. Joshua leaned forward and placed a folder on the table, careful to avoid knocking the pitcher over.

"I did some searches on the name you had. ACB Industries is registered in Tennessee. The owner is listed as a Smaranda Firea."

Reg was delighted to have a name to go with the truffles. But that was quite a name. "I guess there aren't too many of those around."

"No, I don't think so," Josh said seriously. "I had a quick look around, and I couldn't find any in Tennessee."

Reg's heart fell.

"The address given for her here in Tennessee turns out to be a law office," Josh explained.

"So she used her lawyer's address on the registration instead of her own."

He nodded his agreement. "It's not uncommon, particularly with people who don't want to be tracked."

"So it's a dead end."

CHAPTER THIRTY-FIVE

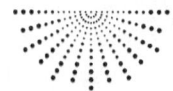

*A*ctually… no. Miss Erin said that you're from Florida? And this is to do with something going on down there?"

Reg nodded. "Yeah. We were hoping to be able to find out who was behind it. If we can't track her down, I don't know how we will stop her."

"I did find a Sma Firea in Florida. Sma is apparently a nickname for Smaranda."

Reg leaned forward. "You found her?" She tried to see the papers that Joshua had.

"I don't know how close we are to physically finding her, but it looks like she lives in Florida." He took a printed page from his folder and handed it to her. "There's an address."

Reg looked down the page, which was a long list of notes from the research Josh had done. Corvin leaned over to look at it and found the information faster than Reg. He pointed at it with a well-manicured nail.

"It's a mailbox," Reg said with disappointment.

"That doesn't mean we can't find her," Corvin told her firmly. "The police can get the records of who owns the box. If it's a private company, the guy who owns the franchise might know her from when she comes to check her box. He'll have contact information. A phone number, email, how she pays for it. We can get that from him."

Reg felt like she had swallowed a bowling ball. A great big, heavy weight sat in her stomach, pushing everything else away, forcing the acid of the lemonade back up her throat. Yes, Corvin could be persuasive. He could use his charms, and if his charms failed, he could use force. She didn't want to be a part of that. But she might have to be.

"Will this be enough for Marta to look into it? She can call this woman and find out if she makes the truffles or gets them from somewhere else. She can figure out who it is in the supply chain that poisoned them. And we won't have to do anything."

"Sure," Corvin agreed smoothly. The others in the room could only hear his words. They couldn't understand, as Reg did, that he was only agreeing because he didn't want to argue with Reg in front of these people. He wanted her to be calm and cooperative and to take him back to Florida, not to leave him stranded there.

Maybe the police would help them out, but they weren't going to jump in quickly and take over just like that. They would take their time to decide to get involved, to get caught up on everyone's backgrounds, and to check the information that Corvin and Reg had found. And eventually, maybe they would get in touch with this Sma woman and have a conversation with her about her truffles. And then what? If she said they were perfectly fine and couldn't have poisoned anybody, would they take her at her word? If she said that it must have been an assistant or deliveryman or even a consumer, who had tainted the truffles, then what could the police do about it? They had to follow the clues. They needed to prove everything one way or the other. And if they said that they had run everything down and hit a dead end, then what?

Then what were Corvin and Reg going to do?

Corvin gave Reg an amused look. So much for not having the argument in front of Erin and Josh. Reg had just summed up the whole thing in her mind. The others were looking at her expectantly. They might not have been able to hear her thoughts as easily as Corvin could, but they could read her face and knew she was not happy with the information she had been given.

Reg needed to go back to Florida. There was work to be done.

"Thank you so much for this information," she told Josh. "Erin was right. You are very good at what you do. I wasn't expecting to have a name and an address so quickly. With this... hopefully, we'll be able to put an end to the killings."

"I'd like to report on the story," Josh said tentatively. "If you could fill me in on the details..."

"No. We can't tell you anything about it until it's resolved. Just like when the police have an active investigation. We don't want to spook this Sma. We need to deal with it quietly."

"And when she's in jail, what about then?"

"I don't know. I'll try to keep you in the loop. But it might take a while. Just because you got us this information, that doesn't mean we'll be able to close the case immediately. It could take..." Reg shrugged and tried to think of what the police would tell her if she asked them for information on an active case. "An investigation can take weeks or months. So... I'm not sure I'll be able to tell you anything soon."

"Well... you remember where you got that information. And who could get you more details if you need more than that."

Reg hoped that they wouldn't need anything else from him. Getting more information without giving him something back in exchange would be difficult. They were lucky that he wasn't an experienced reporter, who would have requested some kind of benefit before giving her the information that she needed.

"Thanks. I'll remember that, and I'll get back to you when I can with the details... however much I can tell you."

"I'm very discreet. I will be very careful what I print. I don't want to jeopardize my sources."

"No, you don't want that." Reg held back a chuckle at his reporter lingo. He was helping her out and he was mature and working on what would be his career when he got out of school, so she had to show him respect. She turned and looked at Corvin. "We'd better get back there."

Corvin nodded his agreement.

"Back to Florida?" Erin asked. "How far did you drive today? You should sleep here and get a good night's rest before starting back again. It's a long way to drive. You don't want to do it tired."

"Better to get a head start today," Reg disagreed. "We're both night people, so we'll get a lot done tonight before either of us is tired."

"Where is your car? Where did you say you had parked?"

"It's not far from here."

Reg was doing her best not to out-and-out lie to Erin, but she couldn't help that one. She apologized to her old friend mentally.

"Let me pack some food for you to take on the road," Erin suggested. "I can whip up some sandwiches for you."

"No, it's okay. We'll get something when we stop for gas."

"Some cookies?" Erin tempted. "Muffins for breakfast tomorrow?"

"Are you determined to make me fat?" Reg demanded. She put her hand over her belly. "Did you notice how much weight I've put on since you saw me last?"

"Maybe a pound or two. But you were too skinny before."

Reg laughed. "Good answer."

Erin was right about Reg being too skinny before, never sure where her next meal was coming from. But wrong about her having gained a pound or two. Maybe a dozen or two.

Reg and Corvin got up and headed for the front door. Erin gave Reg a tight hug and told her goodbye. "This has been a real whirlwind visit. I'd love to be able to see you again when we can really sit down and visit. Do you think you could come for a visit one day?"

Reg could tell Erin she could come to Black Sands whenever she wanted, but she didn't. She didn't want Erin finding out about Reg's magical life there. She wouldn't understand. She would think that Reg was psychotic and that everyone around her was too, or was trying to gaslight her.

"Well... yeah, I'll see if there's some time I could come for a visit," she agreed. Clearly, if she could leave Florida and travel to

Bald Eagle Falls just to find out who owned a company she had read on the back of a bag of truffles, she could visit for something more important, like reconnecting with her sister. "Maybe... Christmas break."

"It would be great if you could come for Christmas," Erin gushed. She gave Reg another hug. "Please do! It would be wonderful to do the holidays together."

As Reg remembered it, Erin didn't do holidays at all. Especially a semi-religious holiday like Christmas. She didn't want anything to do with organized religion. But Erin knew that Reg didn't practice any religion either. They would just be getting together to have a good time. Maybe put up a tree and some decorations, drink eggnog and eat sugar cookies...

It would be fun. She'd like to have Christmas with Erin again.

CHAPTER THIRTY-SIX

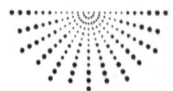

*R*eg was glad they didn't actually have to drive all the way back to Florida. A road trip might be fun, but not that fun. And they were in the midst of a desperate situation, not looking for a fun time. There would be time for road trips later. When they had put a stop to the poisonings in Black Sands.

Reg breathed a sigh of relief when they were out of Erin's house and somewhere quiet so they could jump back to Black Sands. She had been worried that Terry would get home and she would have to deal with a cop breathing down her neck.

He was bound not to like her being back in town and might have a warrant out for her arrest after the last time.

That was one thing she would have to be careful of in returning to visit Erin for Christmas. Erin would have to have a long chat with Officer Terry Piper to make sure there was no possibility of his making trouble for Reg if she went back. She wasn't going back just to be arrested.

Corvin held out his hands to Reg, ready to jump again. Reg took a few deep breaths and made sure that she had everything she needed to take back with her, including the chocolate chocolate chip brownies. She wasn't leaving those behind.

She thought about being home and putting the brownies in the microwave to warm up just a little too clearly and, before she had fully prepared herself for the jump, she was there. Not in the park where Corvin had left the car and Reg had intended to go, but right inside Reg's cottage.

Corvin glanced around the cottage and chuckled, pleased by Reg's mistake.

"And now, my Regina, some time to ourselves." He transferred his grip from her hands to her waist, pulling her closer to him, the scent of roses overpowering. Reg was too slow to resist. Her muscles wouldn't work against this attacker. And she couldn't put her thoughts together quickly enough to know how to protect herself against his charms. It had happened too fast.

Then suddenly, Corvin was gone.

Reg was shocked. She stood there, staring at her empty hands and the open space where he had been standing only an instant earlier.

Starlight jumped up on the counter and meowed at her imperiously. Reg stared at him. "Did *you* do that? What just happened to Corvin?"

"I'm still here," Corvin said. Reg turned around and looked at him, finding him on the opposite side of the room, his cheeks flushed a dusky red. Had Reg sent him there? Was he angry at her because of whatever she had done in a reflex reaction, protecting herself?

But Corvin shifted aside slightly, and Reg saw long legs stretched out behind him. Someone sitting on the couch. Reg couldn't see the whole man because Corvin was blocking her line of vision, but she knew those legs.

"Uncle Harrison!"

"You should not be with the devil incarnate," Harrison said mildly.

Reg hadn't heard Harrison call Corvin *that* before. He must have been watching Netflix.

"I didn't mean to come here. I jumped here accidentally, and he was with me, and… I swear it wasn't on purpose. I meant to jump back to his car."

Harrison shook his head. "A car is not better. A small, enclosed space. You know what could happen."

"I wouldn't have let it."

"You let it here."

Reg couldn't find an argument to that. He was right; Reg had been careless and should not have allowed herself to jump there, shouldn't have put herself in a compromising situation.

"Well, thank you for your help."

Corvin moved to the side slightly so Reg could see Harrison better. The clothes horse had on black and white striped tights, something that Reg had seen him wear before. He must like them. His shirt was a seizure-inducing mix of bright colors. A Hawaiian print. And he wore a skirt. Maybe on a man it was called something different. A leather kilt or loin covering of some sort.

All of this was topped with a wide-brimmed furry hat with long green feathers sprouting out the top.

But Reg didn't take long to admire Harrison's wild sense of fashion. He sat with a bag of truffles in his lap and, while Reg watched, popped one into his mouth.

"Oh! You shouldn't be eating those!" Reg told him, horrified.

Harrison looked curiously into the bag, and then up at Reg. He made a dramatically questioning face. "Are they cat food?" he asked tentatively.

Reg ignored Corvin's chuckles.

"No. No, they're human food, but… we think they might have killed someone. Three people. Four," Reg corrected herself.

"Oh." Harrison nodded understandingly and popped another one into his mouth. "They are very good. We love chocolate."

"They might be poisoned!"

Harrison shrugged, unconcerned. Maybe immortals were not affected by poison like humans were. Reg knew that Harrison only took on a human form for short periods of time. And while he was in human form, who knew whether he actually had internal human physiology, or if his body was just a representation of human anatomy, or even just an illusion.

"We?" she asked.

"We?" Harrison repeated, looking around and trying to figure out what she was talking about.

"You said *we* like chocolate."

"And we do," Harrison agreed.

"Who?" Reg didn't want an unexpected visit from Weston. He and Harrison were a bit much for her to handle all at once. And she suspected that, like two six-year-old boys, they encouraged each other to do things they knew they should not. And full-grown immortals could cause a lot more havoc than a couple of little boys.

"We." Harrison repeated. He pulled a truffle out of the bag and threw it at Reg. It came at her so fast that Reg had no hope of catching it, but ducked to the side to avoid it.

"You—Reg, and I," Harrison said. "We like chocolate."

"Yes, we do," Reg agreed. She picked up the truffle that had fallen to the floor and put it into the garbage can. "I brought us some brownies."

Harrison watched with wide-eyed interest as Reg produced the bag of brownies and put one each for herself and Harrison on a plate. She did not offer Corvin one. He wasn't supposed to be there, and she assumed he would not want to eat something when he didn't know the person who had prepared it. Not after being poisoned at the club and not with the poisoned truffles making their rounds of Black Sands. But Reg trusted Erin's baking, and Harrison would eat anything chocolate. Probably anything she suggested he eat, even if it were fuzzy green caterpillars.

When the brownies were ready, Reg handed one plate to Harrison. He took it from her, and Reg took the bag of truffles from his lap. Sort of like distracting a child by putting a different toy or treat in front of them. Sometimes she thought Harrison little more than a giant toddler in a man's body.

With powerful magic.

Reg sat down with her brownie and used her fork to take a bit. Harrison mirrored her movements and brought the first bite to his own mouth.

"Oooh…" he murmured. "Yes, we like chocolate."

"How many of those truffles did you eat?" Reg asked, looking at the paper bag. She wasn't sure how full it had been to start with. It might have been two-thirds empty, like a cereal box or bag of potato chips. Or he might have eaten a dozen of the treats.

"They didn't count," Harrison said obliquely.

Reg had no idea what he meant. He might have heard it on a TV commercial or movie. Something that a woman said about the calories not counting. It wasn't that Harrison couldn't count. Reg was pretty sure he could. Although facts never seemed to be quite concrete with Harrison. They might change at any time. With the immortals, the past was not unalterable. People's forms, shapes, and nature could all be changed. There was no telling what was real and permanent and what was not. Harrison might have eaten twenty truffles and then decided it was only two, and that might be all it counted for in his reality.

She shook her head and took another bite of the warm brownie. Corvin was watching her in disbelief.

"After all of the sugary baking you have eaten already today…"

"Well…" Reg licked chocolate off of her fingers. "I didn't eat the truffles. That is the important part."

"Reg did not eat the truffles," Harrison chimed in, like the chorus in a Gilbert and Sullivan production, "so she would not die."

CHAPTER THIRTY-SEVEN

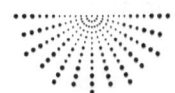

*M*arta agreed to meet Reg and Corvin at The Crystal Bowl once she was finished her shift. It seemed ridiculous that they had to wait until she was off her police shift to discuss police business with her, but Reg kept her mouth shut and just accepted the time that Marta said she was free. There was no point in arguing before they even got to see her. It would be hard enough to convince her that there was a truffle poisoner on the loose in Black Sands.

"Are you going to be ready to eat again by then?" Corvin asked, eyeing the smear of chocolate on Reg's plate.

"That's still a couple of hours away. If I'm not hungry... I'll just have a drink and watch Marta eat. It isn't like we're going there to eat. We're going there to talk."

"There are a lot of places we could go that would be more private."

"We don't *want* more private. We want safe, with plenty of people around in case something were to happen."

She glared at him and didn't indicate what that something might be. It went without saying. Or it should.

"There are other places that would serve as well."

"But we all like The Crystal Bowl. And you're lucky that Marta would even agree to include you in the meeting, so I wouldn't be arguing if I was you."

Corvin shrugged, conceding the point.

Harrison, who usually didn't stick around for long, would not leave until he knew Corvin was out of the house, which Reg greatly appreciated. Nice to have an immortal looking out for her when she hadn't thought she would need him.

Corvin left to get his car, and Reg headed to The Crystal Bowl in her car closer to the time they were supposed to meet. Corvin and Marta were already there ahead of her, Marta looking relaxed and comfortable in Corvin's presence, something that seemed so out of place that Reg was thrown. She looked at Corvin and knew that he was thinking the same thing. Since Marta had found out about her history with Corvin, she had refused to be around him, to speak to him, even to discuss him. If it wasn't the truffles that were affecting her, something was.

"Hi, Reg," Marta greeted her cheerfully. "How are you doing? Corvin says you guys have had a long day. And that he got you up before noon."

"Before eight!"

"Yikes. How are you still awake?"

Reg looked at Corvin. "Lots of sugar and caffeine."

Marta chuckled. She pushed her menu toward Reg. "Are you eating?"

"Maybe something small..." Reg looked down at the menu. Corvin was watching her in amusement. Reg considered her waist-line and decided fries were probably not the best idea. She had consumed quite a few calories already. "Maybe just... a salad and some coffee."

"I don't think I've ever seen you eat a salad," Marta laughed.

"Well... maybe just coffee then." Marta was right. Reg hated salad. If she ordered one, all she would do is push the food around on her plate.

They talked casually until the food arrived, acting as though it was just a regular day and they were only there to socialize. After they had each had several bites—or sips—of their meals, Reg decided it was time to introduce the topic of conversation that they were actually there for.

"So… I guess you know all about Helen Papadakis's death by now. Beverley Bartley's twin sister."

"Were they twins? I didn't realize that." Marta continued to eat without any apparent interest in the topic.

"Yeah. And we think she was poisoned by the same thing as Beverley and the others."

Reg waited for a dramatic reaction. Marta choking on her food or shouting that the deaths were all unrelated and that there was no killer. But she just continued to eat as though unconcerned.

"Those truffles that you asked them to send back with the body."

"Right," Reg agreed.

"Neat trick, by the way, to get them in for testing. Once they were identified as a potential source of a toxin and arrived at the medical examiner's office with the body, they had to test them."

Reg sighed in relief. "Great! What did they find?"

"Well, most tox reports take several weeks to get in. It isn't like it is on TV. And you have to know what kind of poison you are looking for. Antifreeze or eyedrops or rat poison. They'll test for the top street drugs and accidental poisoning toxins, but anything rare… they have to know what they're looking for."

"But we don't know what we're looking for."

"No. They did some quick tests for opioids or other things we have rapid tests for, but nothing showed up."

"So it could be another poison. Just something rare. It could be… some botanical poison that someone grew in their garden. Or…" Reg trailed off.

"Or it could be a charm or spell," Corvin inserted, "which isn't going to show up in any of your lab tests."

Marta nodded her agreement. "No way to test for those. Some practitioners can sense them but, if neither of you could…" Marta motioned back and forth between Corvin and Reg. "Then there probably isn't anything there. Or anything detectable, anyway."

She took a large bite of her burger and said nothing else for a few minutes.

"But you don't even know whether those truffles were poisoned. Or if all of them were, or just a few. Or if the people who died were actually poisoned." She chewed slowly. "We need a lot more evidence before we can pursue this line of investigation. The truffles are being tested further, but do you think they will find anything?"

Reg weighed her words. "We think… they might be affecting your judgment."

CHAPTER THIRTY-EIGHT

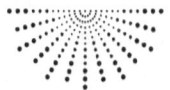

$\mathcal{M}$arta stopped chewing. "*My* judgment?"

"You've been eating the truffles, haven't you?"

"Like everyone else. That's the other thing. If they were all tainted, then you would expect a lot more deaths, wouldn't you? Not just a few random ones? It doesn't seem likely that the truffles were all poisoned. If they weren't, then it must just have been a few. And those ones have all been eaten now. So we don't need to worry about it."

"You see?" Reg pointed out. "You don't even care. You don't think there is anything going on, and you don't think there is anything to be worried about. The family members all seemed to just accept the deaths and didn't act like they were grieving. We think that whatever is in the truffles dampens your emotions—"

"Different people grieve differently," Marta said, shaking her head. "One thing we are taught as detectives is that there is no right or wrong response to a sudden death. People have been rail-roaded by cops who thought that they didn't act the right way to a death notification. It's confirmation bias. You think that the person didn't act upset enough, so you start looking at them through a different lens. You see everything that suggests it was them and nothing that suggests it wasn't."

"That's not what we're talking about here. *None* of them seemed terribly upset by the deaths."

"I can assure you, they were, even if they didn't show it."

"Then why didn't any of them show it? I can see one person holding back their emotions or not acting like it meant as much to them as it did. But all of them? And you, wouldn't you normally be all over this? Four deaths in the magical community in such a short period of time? Those truffles being blanketed all over the town. Have you looked into the distributor at all? Doesn't it seem strange that they would suddenly be in every store and restaurant in town? That everyone would love them and be eating them?"

"Except you two," Marta said, looking at Reg and Corvin. "So why didn't the two of you have any? I happen to know that Reg likes chocolate." Marta smiled, "And I've seen *you* eat small treats like that before," she told Corvin. "So what's with the two of you? Why wouldn't you eat them?"

"I was on vacation," Reg reminded her. "And I actually don't like truffles very much. They're too rich."

"Too rich? You should try these ones. They're much better than any of the mainstream truffles. They are light and creamy and—" Marta had pulled a nearly-consumed bag of truffles out of her pocket. "You really should try them!"

Reg couldn't help but be horrified that not only did Marta not think that there might be any danger in the truffles, but that she was carrying them around to eat them and offering them to other people. What if she poisoned someone else? What if she were eating the ones found at Helen's house? Why was everyone who ate the truffles so intent on feeding them to everyone else?

Reg looked at Corvin for help, trying to figure out where to go next with the conversation. She didn't know if there was a way to get Marta to believe that the truffles were poisoned. If four deaths didn't do it, then what would it take? She obviously didn't believe they were affecting her, much less likely to kill her.

"Reg and I did some research on where the truffles came from," Corvin told Marta. "We figured that way, you would be able to track down the culprit and ask them some questions about what is in the truffles and what might be making people sick."

"Well, since there's no proof that the truffles are making anyone sick, I'm not sure what good it will do. I think that if the truffles were a problem, there would be a lot more casualties." She shrugged. "Like you said, everyone is eating them. So if they were a problem, everyone would be sick."

"Not if there are only a small percentage of people that they make sick, or she was able to target a small subset of people…"

"She?"

"Sma Firea."

"Sma… what?" Marta looked baffled.

"Smaranda Firea," Reg said. "The owner of the company that produces the truffles. Probably the head baker. Or chocolatier or whatever you call them. Quite possibly the witch who is poisoning Black Sands."

She knew that her words were overly dramatic, but she felt like the only way she would reach Marta was by being dramatic. If her emotions were being dampened by the truffles, then Reg needed to push harder to reach her.

Despite her objections to the idea of the truffles being poisoned, Marta leaned forward and looked intrigued. "You know who the maker of the truffles is? I thought it was some out-of-tower. The package says they're from South Virginia or something." Marta turned her bag to find the information on it.

"ACB Industries in Tennessee," Reg informed her. "We went there to look her up. But even though the company is registered in Tennessee, the owner is actually right here."

Marta's mouth hung open. "You went to Tennessee to find out?"

"Exactly. We're both really concerned about this. I'm sure you are, too, even if you need more proof. If we can just help you to gather the evidence you need to prove that Firea is the one who is trying to poison everyone, then you can move forward to arrest her. Once you have enough."

Marta nodded slowly. "Right…" she agreed, voice tentative and uncertain.

Reg pulled the paper out of her skirt pocket and unfolded it. "Here is the address. Do you know her?"

Marta was faster than Reg at finding the information on the page, even though Reg had looked at it once before. "I don't remember seeing her or running across that name before."

"You've never had to arrest her for anything else? She doesn't have a record?"

"I'd have to look her up to be sure that she didn't have a record. Some people get one or two charges and then straighten up or avoid the limelight so we don't see them again. I wouldn't know if she's that kind until I do a database search. That will show whether she's been arrested before. And possibly also if she has a record in another part of the country." Marta smoothed the paper. "It can be challenging, especially with practitioners. Things get too hot in one part of the country, and they change their name and pop up some-where else, a new person."

Reg certainly knew all about that. How many different names and towns had she burned through before finally landing in Black Sands?

"The name is unique," Marta said. "It might be her real name. I don't know any other Fireas, though. Do you?" She directed the query at Corvin. Obviously, Reg wasn't likely to know anyone in Black Sands that Marta hadn't run into a few times before.

"Old family name," Corvin mused. "I don't know when the last time I saw it was. Seems to me they lived pretty deep in the woods. You might ask Davyn. He might have run into her."

"Because he was the coven leader?" Reg asked.

"Because it sounds like a firecaster name. If she is a firecaster… it would be good to know that before anyone confronts her."

"I thought she was your kind," Reg objected. "I was under the impression that witches or warlocks living out in the middle of the forest like hermits were more likely to be… like you."

Corvin looked at Marta as if this wasn't something he had

wanted her to hear. Reg pressed her lips together. She should have kept her mouth shut.

"There is that possibility," he agreed. "My kind are known for being outcasts. Being forced to live away from other people."

"And lurking in the forest luring young children or innocent travelers," Marta added. She didn't say it like it personally offended her, as she often did, but in a flat, distant tone. Like she was talking about someone who had lived a long time ago and in a faraway land. Just a fairy tale. Maybe Corvin was the only power drinker Marta had ever known personally. His race was dying out. There couldn't be that many of them living in hideaways in the woods.

"You know that kind of story is just meant to inflame people against my kind," Corvin said sharply. "I wouldn't expect you to be one reinforcing the old prejudices, Marta."

Marta considered this, staring him in the eyes. Eventually, she dropped her gaze. "You're right. I haven't personally known any hermits who carried your curse. Maybe it is just an old wives' tale."

"We should still be careful," Reg warned. "We should know what kind of a witch she is before approaching her."

Marta and Corvin both nodded. This was, at least, not something anyone could argue with. They couldn't very well advocate for going in blind.

Reg laughed.

Corvin and Marta looked at her, curious.

"I'm always the cautious one," Reg deadpanned.

Corvin smiled. "Yes, you've always been the one to slow everyone down and make them consider the consequences."

Marta didn't laugh as she normally would, but just shook her head at their jokes.

"You're going to come with us, right?" Reg asked. "When we go to find out who this witch is and where she lives? Find out why she would be making poisoned truffles?"

"You are not police or agents of the police."

"No. That's why we should have you around. For some legitimacy. And so that we have some threat to hold over her. If we go to talk to her and we have a cop there, she at least knows that she could be arrested. And you can threaten to get a warrant or a subpoena or whatever you need in that kind of circumstance."

"I don't have any reason to investigate this woman. Like I said, we don't even have any proof that—"

"It's the best lead that we've got right now. We have to follow it up. You don't want to sit around doing nothing. When the media gets wind of this, if it looks like the police haven't been doing anything, the department will end up with a real black eye."

"My boss hasn't authorized opening an investigation into these deaths as homicides. They are natural deaths. They're for the medical examiner's office to investigate. We need to leave it to them until the medical examiner says that they are homicides."

Reg shook her head, trying to find her way through Marta's roadblocks. She closed her eyes, trying to read Marta's thoughts and what method would get her cooperation.

"Listen… didn't you tell me that the medical examiner and the police work in partnership?"

"Yes, exactly."

"And the evidence you bring to the medical examiner influences their determination."

Marta was hesitant. "In some cases."

"Like, he can't always tell if it was a heart attack or an allergy, or poisoning. But if you tell him there is this empty bottle of pills on the bedside table, or their roommate said they were allergic to peanuts and there was an open jar of peanut butter in the kitchen, all of those things help him to make a determination as to the cause of death." Reg's spirits lifted as she was sure she nailed the argument.

"Yes," Marta agreed. "He has to know everything relevant about the scene and what we find out about their life. He takes all of that into account."

Reg nodded happily. "So if you don't tell him that everyone was eating these truffles before they died, he doesn't know it's part of why they died. But if you brought him evidence that they were dangerous, it would help him to make a decision. And if he told you that the truffles could be part of what killed them, then you would have to investigate them further, right?"

Corvin sat back in his chair, grinning at Reg. Reg tried not to look too proud of herself. She was just making a suggestion. It was Marta who would actually make the decision. She was the one who knew how it worked and would decide how to proceed with the investigation.

"What makes you think it is the truffles?" she finally asked.

CHAPTER THIRTY-NINE

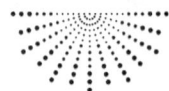

*I*t was too late to do much that night. Marta had already been on shift all day. She needed to get some rest before she could proceed with the investigation. The next day, she would need to look Sma Firea up in the police and municipal databases to try to track down where she lived and what her background was.

Reg had been up way too long and knew she would be forced to wake up before noon again the next day for them to have the best chance of finding Sma Firea and establishing whether she was guilty of poisoning people all over Black Sands.

Marta still held on to the hope that they would find out the truffles were not poisoned. It was something else. Accidental poisoning by some other means, or natural causes as they had first thought. But Reg talked about the other Shoop children and how Marta would feel if another of them were to die. And other children in other families. They couldn't just let innocent people die because Marta didn't want to believe the truffles were poisoned.

Reg's phone rang way too early the next morning. She had slept, at least. Slept like the dead, in fact. When she picked up her phone, she could see that she had missed several other calls and texts before waking up.

She cleared her throat and answered hoarsely. "Hello."

"About time you woke up," Corvin said. "We didn't think we were ever going to raise you. Marta is on her way over to pick you up. Figured it would be best to send her, because she can at least get into the house and wake you up if you hadn't managed to get out of bed yet. She's on her way over now."

Reg stumbled out of bed, holding the phone in one hand and rubbing her eyes with the other. "Okay, okay. I'm up. I'd better go so I'm ready when she gets here."

"See you soon," Corvin agreed, and ended the call. Reg was glad that he got off so quickly. He was one of those people who tended to keep her on the phone and drew out goodbyes as long as possible. But she supposed it was different when they would see each other in a few minutes anyway. Keeping her on the phone would actually delay his being able to see her.

Reg splashed water on her face and used the facilities. She quickly ran a toothbrush around her mouth and headed for the coffee machine. That was the most critical part of her morning routine. She wasn't going anywhere without her coffee.

Starlight intercepted her, meowing and rubbing around her ankles. He seemed to think that the most important part of the morning was feeding him. Reg laughed and dished him out some leftover casserole while she waited for the machine to spit out her morning java.

"You think I should feed you?" she teased. "You think that's what I need to be reminded to do before I leave this morning?"

Starlight nipped her bare ankle.

"Ouch! Hey!" Reg swatted him away. "No biting! What do you think this is? You don't bite me!"

He made a grunting, growling sound and stayed out of her reach.

"Maybe I won't give you any food," Reg said. "Maybe you'll think again about biting me."

He sat up straight like a sphinx and stared at her. Reg could feel him reaching out to her, commanding her to feed him. And she wanted to. She knew she couldn't leave without feeding him; it hadn't been a serious threat.

"I'll feed you. But you can't bite me. I don't know why you did that."

She scooped the casserole into his dish, keeping an eye on him in case he decided to sneak up and bite again. But he didn't; he just sat there staring at her. Reg wondered if it was because he knew she was going out somewhere with Corvin. He had never liked Corvin.

"Here you go." Reg put the bowl down on the floor. "And I'm not going with him alone, you know. I'm going with Marta. We have to find out about this witch that's killing people. You wouldn't want her to kill Sarah or another witch you know, would you? We have to put a stop to it."

He blinked his eyes slowly, leaving them squinted into long slits for a few seconds.

"You wouldn't want me to let a bunch of innocent people die. I have to save them, just like you and Horace were saving the people that the cabal was targeting. I know you care about innocent people being attacked or killed."

He lowered his position, so that he crouched like a long, round loaf instead of sitting up straight. He looked at his food bowl.

"Eat," Reg told him. "I'm sorry I threatened you. I was just upset by you biting me."

Eventually, he stood up, padded over to his food bowl, and started eating. Reg looked down at herself after filling her coffee to-go cup.

"I guess I'd better get dressed too. Can't exactly go wandering around Black Sands in my pajamas."

Even though her pajamas were just a short and t-shirt set. Not a matching set. Just two old, wrinkled, holey articles of clothing. They were comfy. But they were not for walking around town in.

She hurried to get on a headdress, shirt, and skirt. It wouldn't take Marta long to get there. She might already be parking out front.

Reg was just putting on a couple of necklaces to complete her outfit when Marta texted to say she was waiting outside. Corvin must have told her he'd managed to wake Reg up, because she didn't ask. She grabbed her handbag, said goodbye to Starlight, and headed out to the car.

She stopped at the gate to the front yard and stayed behind the fence line as she looked out into the street for Marta's car. It was waiting there, as promised. But Reg waited, straining her eyes to see the person in the driver's seat and mentally commanding Marta to turn her head. In a moment, Marta did so, looking toward the gate to see if Reg was coming. She raised her hand in greeting.

After seeing her face to confirm that it was actually her in the car, Reg left the safety of the backyard and got into Marta's car.

"Bright and early," Marta teased.

"I'm here."

"It's like the middle of the night for you."

Reg nodded her agreement. "Coffee," she said, putting her travel mug into the cup holder. "Lots of coffee."

CHAPTER FORTY

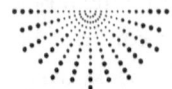

They met Corvin at a crossroad near the physical address Marta had found for Sma's house.

"We ready to do this?" Reg asked.

Everyone nodded. Marta looked around at the wooded surroundings. "Pretty dense here. It's not going to be easy to find her. The houses out here aren't exactly marked properly. They've all been given addresses, but it isn't like a grid system where they are all lined up in a predictable order. Some of them are very... off-road."

"What about GPS?"

"I have the GPS coordinates marked, but..." Marta trailed off.

Reg looked at her and then at Corvin. "But what? The GPS coordinates let you find exactly where it is, don't they?"

"If they're correct," Marta agreed. "They aren't always. And sometimes houses are moved or replaced. This is sort of... the Bermuda Triangle of Black Sands. Things... disappear out here."

"Right here?" Reg looked around uneasily. She had been in the Everglades and had seen how things disappeared or seemed to move from one place to another, never in the same location twice. As exciting as it was to think about finding something that had been lost, like a plane that had crashed decades earlier, being lost and worrying that someone else might not find *her* for a few more decades was not nearly so nice.

Marta looked at her phone and pointed. "It should be over there. I'll lead." She glanced over at Corvin. "Follow closely. Don't lose sight of us. Don't *blink*."

"That might be a little extreme." He smiled at her tolerantly. "I assure you, I'm not going to get lost."

"You'd better not."

They returned to their vehicles and drove along the road slowly. Marta braked a couple of times and searched for a break in the foliage. "There should be a road around here somewhere."

"I don't see anything. Maybe it is farther away than it looks. Sometimes the GPS is wonky. It looks like something is close when it's still half a mile away."

Marta watched the screen of her phone, waiting tensely for the map to shift and show that they had gone past the turnoff. In a moment, the screen redrew, and they seemed to be looking at a different map altogether. They reached a crossroad and looked at the signage.

"We went too far," Marta sighed.

"How could we? There was nowhere to turn. There was no house. Turn in here. Maybe there's an access road off of this one that goes that way."

"We can't just drive around randomly. We'll get lost and won't be able to find our way back out."

"It isn't a labyrinth. Just try it. If we don't see a house, we'll come right back out this way."

Marta pulled into the access road and drove a short distance down. There was no other road branching off to the right. They reached a farmhouse. Blue with white trim. Old and dilapidated. Paint peeling.

"That's not it," Marta said, looking at the house and then at a picture or address on her phone.

"Well, we can ask here. They'll be able to tell us how to get there."

Reg opened her door and got out. Corvin's car pulled in behind Marta and he opened his door. "This isn't it."

"I know. I'm just going to ask here."

Reg went up to the house. She could feel Corvin's warning not to, but she couldn't see how there could be anything wrong with asking. The worst that could happen was that there would be no one home or they would not talk to her and they would continue on to the next house instead. Sooner or later, they would figure out where she was.

The door opened partway before Reg lifted her hand to knock on it, and a woman looked out. She was taller than Reg, a brunette, wearing an old-style apron with sleeves and pockets.

"Who are you?"

"My name is Reg. I'm looking for Sma, but I can't find the access road. Am I in the right place?"

"She doesn't live here."

"No, I know that. I meant... can you point me in the right direction? The GPS isn't right and I don't know where the access road is."

"You can't get there from here."

"Which way do I need to go?"

"Back out to the highway."

"And...?"

"Find it from there."

"I will... if I can... but it's not showing up. It's over that way?" Reg gestured.

"That's what the map says."

"Well... maps can be wrong."

The woman looked at her and Reg didn't know if it was because the woman thought she had said something wise or stupid.

"Sma does not encourage visitors."

"We need to talk to her. There's been some trouble."

The house owner didn't ask, "What kind of trouble?" Like Reg thought she would. She just shook her head. "You should leave Sma alone. Stay away from her."

"Is she the one who makes those delicious truffles? Or does she just sell them?"

"Truffles?"

"Those chocolates she makes. They really are delicious, aren't they?"

"I don't know what you're talking about."

The woman closed the door in her face. Reg went back to the car. "She said to go back out to the highway and try again from there."

Marta growled in the back of her throat and put the car into gear. "I could have told you that."

"Sorry. I thought she would have better directions. They *are* neighbors."

"Did she admit to that?"

"Well… not exactly. But she knew Sma. Talked about her."

"That's something."

They went back to the highway and repeated the process, this time ending up at the other side of where the house should be. Reg had to knock on this door, a number of hard bashes before someone finally came to see what the racket was about.

"Get out of here," a little old man with a shotgun told her. "No trespassing."

"I'm not trespassing. I'm trying to find Sma's place. Can you tell me how to get to it from here?"

"Sma don't like people. Neither do I. Get on your way."

"We need to talk to her. Is it this way? Is it hidden somewhere nearby?"

"You'd best stay away from her."

"Is she known for being a bad neighbor? What exactly do you think she's going to do to me?"

"She doesn't want anything to do with anyone. And the town…" The old man shook his head. "Those people have been messing around, getting Sma all riled up. She's been *quiet* for years, but now…"

"What people?"

"The town."

"People in Black Sands?"

"The Town. Town of Black Sands. In the pockets of all of the developers. They take the land."

Reg tried to make sense of it. "The town is trying to build out here?"

He nodded. "Widen the highway. Put in a new development or two. Get rid of the old folks who have lived here for centuries."

"They're expropriating the land?" Corvin had come up behind Reg without her hearing him, and his question made her jump.

"Taking it right away from everyone," the old man agreed. "Think that by paying us a few pennies, they can do whatever they want. Take people off of the land that's belonged to the family for centuries."

"I didn't know they could do that," Reg said.

The man pounded his fist into his hand. "That backstabbing mayor! He comes from old stock. Told us oldsters that he would never do something like this. Then the weasel goes and does just what he said he never would. Says he couldn't help it. The pressures of development. The good of Black Sands."

The old man spat.

"If we wanted to be part of Black Sands, we would have moved there. None of us want to be part of a new development. To have to give up our family homes. I was born in this house. My *grandpa* was born in this house."

"That's awful. How can they do that?"

"You ask that traitor. He comes from old stock. A distant cousin of Sma. She said that he would stand by the family, that he would protect us from all of their machinations. Now look at it. Soon they'll be out here with bulldozers to knock everything down and make way for the new development. New! Who wants a *new* house? Those things are monstrosities."

"Where is Sma? Do you think I could talk to her? Find out what she thinks about all of this?"

"I'll tell you what she thinks of it. She thinks that he's a traitor and a weasel. She'd as soon slit the man's throat as shake his hand."

Reg swallowed. They were getting close to an answer. Was Sma that angry at the town? Betrayed and angry about the whole thing? Angry enough that she would want to kill anyone she could? Completely shut down the town so they wouldn't proceed with the construction or the demolition that would precede it?

CHAPTER FORTY-ONE

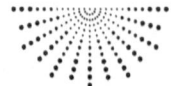

*Y*ou have to know how to get there," the man told her. "You can't just drive in."

"There's no road?"

He shook his head. "Not usually."

Reg wasn't sure what "not usually" meant. But she knew what "no road" meant. It meant they would have to hike in. There was no other way. They couldn't drive through the dense trees without a road.

"What's the best way to get to her house?" Reg asked. He had said that they had to know how to get there. Who knew how long it would take them if they didn't have proper directions. They might be wandering out there all day. Or for half of eternity.

"If Sma did not invite you, there is no point in looking for it."

"The mayor or the people from the town must have been able to find it to tell her it was being expropriated."

"The mayor could," the old man agreed, rubbing his chin thoughtfully. "Maybe because they were distant kin. You never know what doors blood will open."

"We really need to talk to her."

"You're welcome to try, honey." The man made a vague motion to his right. "You'll find her—or not find her—at Two Springs, near the waterfall. Whether you can get there or not... I guess that depends on you."

Reg looked at the others. "I guess we try it? We've got the GPS coordinates. Maybe they'll work better if we're on foot instead of trying to drive in. If the road is only there sometimes, that would explain not being able to find it on the phone map."

"You're not exactly dressed for hiking through the woods," Corvin pointed out.

Reg looked at her skirt and sandals. "It's pretty much what I wore tramping around Erin's woods yesterday. I survived that."

"There might be poison ivy."

"Oh," the old man chortled. "You can be sure there's poison ivy."

"I can do it," Reg insisted. "We need to find her, put a stop to the deaths."

Corvin nodded his agreement. "If you think you can manage it." He turned his gaze to Marta. "You're pretty pale today, Mar— Detective Jessup. Are you okay for a hike?"

"I'm just fine. I'm in as good a shape as anyone. Better than you, sitting around with your books all day."

Corvin snorted. "I'm just trying to look out for your welfare. To be sensitive to your needs."

"What I could really use right now," Marta wiped her glistening forehead with the back of her hand. Reg expected her to express her desire for a nice cold drink, whether it was lemonade or something harder. "Is one of those dang truffles."

Reg didn't know what to say to that. Marta threw her an angry look.

"Yeah, that's right, I stopped eating them because of you. And I feel like crap. I really could use a pick-me-up about now."

Her pallor and irritability were withdrawal from the truffles, then. Reg wondered again what could be in them. Was it chemically based and could be found by the police lab? Or was it magical, something that would defy all of their tests?

"This way?" Reg pointed in the direction the old man had indicated. "That's where we'll find her house?"

"If you can find it," he agreed.

* * *

They probably should have taken compass bearings. If the old man's gesture had been accurate, and there was nothing to say that it had been. Reg quickly found herself turned around and wondering how large or small the house might be. Had they walked right by it? Could it be hidden in the trees, just behind a hill or grove of trees too thick to see anything through? Was it a tiny shack or a sprawling mansion? How much magic was actually in place to protect her from unwanted guests?

They followed the GPS directions on Marta's phone for an hour. Reg was sure they had approached it from every direction, and yet it eluded them at every turn.

"This isn't working," Reg grumbled. "How did we expect modern technology to trump magic? This is as bad as chasing around the woods after that stupid crow."

"Crows are not stupid," Corvin said stiffly.

"That wasn't really my point."

"A crow would be able to find the house."

Reg glared at him. "Then why don't you ask a crow to take you there."

They stared at each other for a few seconds. Then Corvin raised his brows and looked around. Reg suddenly became aware of the birds in the trees and other creatures in the wood around them. They might be hiding out of sight, but they were there. And Corvin was probably right; they knew exactly where the house was and how to get there. The house had been there for decades or centuries.

She could feel Corvin reaching out, trying to communicate with the birds around him, looking for the one crow or other corvid that he would be able to communicate his desires too. Reg was not the best at communicating with birds, but she did her best to boost Corvin's signal, trying to communicate what they needed. She didn't know how much a bird could understand about what they were doing. If it had been Starlight, she would have described their intentions and the consequences of not being able to find the witch in full. But could the birds understand the threat of what could happen in the future? The possibility of so many people dying—innocent men, women, and children?

Eventually, it seemed like the rest of the forest around them quieted, and Reg heard the cawing of a single crow off in the distance. She looked at Corvin, and he nodded. "We might as well try."

The three of them followed the sound, eventually reaching the tree that the crow perched in above them. As soon as they got close, it flapped its wings and took off, taking up another perch several trees away, out of sight. Reg followed Corvin as he chased after the bird, but she was worried. It seemed to be leading them deeper into the woods, always staying ahead of them, always out of sight. It could be some trick. It could be the witch herself trying to lead them to their deaths. It could be a guard who had shifted into bird form. Or an actual bird enchanted to lead people deeper into the forest, to their eventual deaths.

"Pleasant thoughts," Corvin muttered to Reg.

"Sorry."

"Trust the guide we have been given."

"Okay."

Her legs were getting scratched up by the undergrowth, and she remembered Corvin's warning about poison ivy. She really hoped they wouldn't have to deal with that at the end of their journey. She'd gotten poison ivy on a youth camping trip once.

She hated camping.

CHAPTER FORTY-TWO

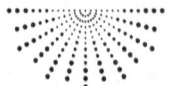

$\mathcal{C}$orvin looked over his shoulder at her again, and Reg tried to eliminate the negative thoughts and just focus on their trek through the woods. At least they had a guide and were no longer relying on modern technology to find the witch's ancient hiding place. Eventually, the bird would lead them to its destination, whatever that was. There would be an end to their journey, one way or the other.

"Can we stop for a break?" Marta asked.

Reg was surprised she had been the one to ask. Out of the three of them, she would have expected Marta to be the one in the best shape, out and about on patrol and doing her various police duties each day, while Corvin tended to be reading and Reg was, quite frankly, too lazy to get any exercise and preferred to be curled up on the couch watching videos on her phone when she was not dealing with clients or taking care of chores or errands that she couldn't get out of.

Corvin nodded and stopped. Reg saw that he was sweating, his face flushed. Despite what he had said to her, he wasn't exactly dressed for a hike either, his black cloak adding an extra layer he didn't need, absorbing the rays of the sun. It must have been sweltering, yet he hadn't taken it off and draped it over his arm or tied it around his waist. Maybe Reg's flowy skirt and sandals hadn't been such a bad idea.

They stood around, looking at each other and catching their breaths. Reg thought about Sma Firea and stretched out her senses, looking at the woods around her and trying to build a picture of the house in her mind. How did it look to the crow? Did his bird's eye view allow him to see her house clearly, or was it hidden under a thick canopy of trees? Was Sma a bird person or did she prefer another animal? Or no animals at all? It would be a lonely existence if she didn't get along with any people or animals.

Something else was added to the picture that she hadn't been expecting.

"I smell water," Reg said.

Corvin and Marta sniffed at the air and both shook their heads.

"Your siren senses," Corvin said, "you're much more sensitive to it than we are."

"The old man said it was at Two Springs by the waterfall," Jessup reminded her. "So if you can find one of the springs that feeds into the waterfall…"

Reg nodded. She sniffed, breathing the tiny airborne water molecules deeper into her lungs. "It's this way."

Forgetting about the rest break, Reg followed her nose, leading the others toward the waterfall. Reg knew it was the waterfall itself she had smelled rather than just one of the springs feeding into it. The waterfall threw copious amounts of spray up into the air, and that was what she was smelling. It was fresh and clean and awakened a thirst in Reg that was more than just the need to drink. This was a thirst that could not be satisfied by coffee or juice.

She led them quickly through glades and denser brush, until Corvin and Marta, too, could hear the rushing water and smell the spray in the air. Reg headed directly for the waterfall, forgetting all about the witch and her house for the time being.

"Reg!" Corvin called, concerned about her running ahead of the group.

"You'd better stay back, Corvin," she warned. If he got too close to her when her siren instincts were triggered or tried to stop her from reaching her goal, things would not go well for him.

Corvin had the wisdom to do what she said instead of arguing that he had the power to protect himself from her. He knew only too well how susceptible he was to sirens. It didn't matter how much power he had; when her venom touched his skin, it put an end to his free will.

Reg burst through the trees to a clearing where the two streams joined and the resulting flow of water fell over a series of stepped rocks. Rainbows appeared in the spray as she moved closer, an ethereal shimmer in the air.

She ignored everything else and knelt by the pool at the bottom of the falls, scooping the frigid water into her palm to drink it and splash it on her face. Her senses were a hundred times sharper than usual. It was like looking through a microscope and binoculars at the same time. Everything was crystal clear, both close at hand and far away, and the same was true of all of her senses.

Corvin and Marta stayed back at the tree line, keeping themselves hidden from any observers and giving Reg the space she needed. She could smell Corvin's intoxicating odor—not his rose-scented pheromones, but sweat from the walk and the hot sun and the blood that pumped below the surface. But he was far enough away that she could control herself.

They stood back, waiting for Reg to finish. In a few minutes, her thirst was slaked. Reg stood up and looked around.

"This is the waterfall. Where is the house?"

"There may be more than one waterfall," Corvin pointed out.

Reg circled the area, watching for signs of human habitation. Not just the house itself, but footprints or trampled areas, a candle or altar, a garden or food offered to the animals that lived there.

There was a large, flat rock that might have been used as an altar. The earth around it was compacted, but it was impossible to tell whether it had been trampled by human feet or animals. In a clearing, Reg found a few peanuts that might have been dropped by a bird or squirrel. Peanuts were grown in Florida, but not in the woods, where the dense canopy cut out much of the sunlight. That meant a human had brought it into the area at some point. Corvin's bird friend had brought them closer to the house, so maybe the witch fed them and the birds knew it as a friendly place.

"We're close," she told Corvin and Marta.

They didn't say anything. Reg looked up and toward them. A child stood before Corvin and Marta, gazing up at them. Reg blinked. She circled around the clearing to get a better look at the gamin. It was a boy, as far as Reg could tell, with a dirty face and tattered clothes. He was pale and thin, but his eyes were bright and alert.

"Who are you?" Reg asked.

The child looked at her. "You shouldn't be here."

"I know. We're probably trespassing. But we wanted to talk to Sma Firea. Can you tell her that we're looking for her? Guide us to her house?"

"You are not welcome here. Only those who are invited may go further."

"Then invite us," Reg said impatiently. "We need to talk to her. Is she your boss? Your mother?"

"Sma has no attachments."

"Well, that's convenient, isn't it? She doesn't need to follow anyone else's rules if it's just her living in the wilderness by herself."

"You must leave." The child's large, hollow eyes were nearly black. There was hardly any white around the iris, making him look like a zombie or some other creature.

"I don't want to leave. Invite us to the house. Then we can talk to Sma and get this all straightened out."

Even as they conversed, Reg was trying to figure the child out. She couldn't get any emotions from him. It was like he was some kind of robot left there to guard against intruders. But he was creepy. Reg didn't like the flat, blank eyes. He was human but not human.

They must be close to the entrance of the house, or there wouldn't be anyone there to guard against trespassers. They had broken through all of the outer defenses. They were in the right place. And now they were poised to gain entrance if she could trigger the right sequence or say the magic word. She went over the conversation in her head to see if the guard had said anything to her in a code that was supposed to give her a clue to the words to say to get in. In the movies, that was always how it worked.

"Do you like truffles?" she asked the child. "Do you want something to eat?"

He turned his hollow eyes to her. "Truffles?" he repeated.

"Do you like truffles? Mystical Morsels?" It made sense that one of these words might be the trigger that would get them audience with Smaranda Firea. "ACB Industries?"

There was a clicking from the child. "Truffles?"

"Yes. Chocolate truffles. They are delicious and... mysterious." Reg tried to think of what else had been on the paper bags of truffles. The ingredients. There had been some kind of blurb telling people how wonderful the truffles were. "Mystical Morsels. Chocolate Truffles. Making all of your dreams come true. Light and creamy. The perfect blend of... something and something. Made by ACB Industries. Distributed by ACB Industries. Tennessee."

"They're addictive," Marta chimed in, trying to help Reg. "They're to die for."

There was another click from the child. "Truffles," he repeated. "They're to die for."

"I wish we'd brought some with us," Reg said. "Do you think we're supposed to give him a truffle to eat?"

"I wouldn't think so," Corvin said, but he didn't sound too certain about his supposition.

The child held his hand out to Reg. Not for payment or a truffle, but for her to hold it. Reg looked at the others. "You'd better stay with me."

"We will," Marta assured her.

"We'll do our best," Corvin said.

Which didn't make Reg feel a lot better about walking away with the child, or whatever he really was. A robot? A zombie? He didn't look like a pixie. But he didn't feel like a human.

CHAPTER FORTY-THREE

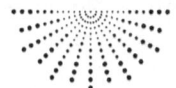

"Come," the child urged, holding his hand out insistently.

Reg took a deep breath in and let it out again. She put her hand into the little one, sure she was about to be transported to some location where Corvin and Marta could not follow her. But she was still there. The child tugged on her hand, and Reg followed, one step at a time, checking over her shoulder frequently to see if the others were still with her. They followed at a distance, though they were gradually closing in, catching up to Reg a little more every few steps. The child didn't try to stop them, and they did not run into an invisible barrier they could not cross.

After a short walk through the woods, Reg could make out a house through the trees.

"Finally," she murmured. She looked back at Corvin. He kept following.

They reached another clearing. The grass was short. Not an even canvas like a lawn that had been cut with a lawn mower, but wilder, more like a meadow. Maybe one where goats had been grazing. She remembered the goats at Bella's farm in Tennessee.

The house that stood in the middle of the field was stunning. Reg had been expecting little more than a shack, similar to what the neighbors had. Old houses with wood frames and siding and paint peeling off.

But the house in front of her was the gingerbread house of fairy tales. Dark, almost chocolate-brown walls, with white lacy trim pierced with eyelets and embellished with scrollwork. It was not actual gingerbread and icing, but it looked good enough to eat.

She looked behind her. Corvin and Marta were right there, almost on top of her. Ready to go inside with her when the door opened. It was comforting to have them at her back, ready to face whatever opened the door.

Reg was thirsty again, her mouth as dry as cotton.

The boy mounted the white-painted stairs onto the porch and knocked on the door to announce himself. He did not wait for an answer, but turned the door handle, pushed the door open, and pulled Reg into the house.

Reg froze once inside the door.

The child was gone. He had been holding her hand, and then he wasn't. She supposed he had returned to wherever he had been before appearing to her by the waterfall.

"Where did he go?" she asked the room in general.

It was sparsely decorated. Nothing looked too shabby or too new. It looked as if it had been decorated two hundred years ago and since then had been preserved, untouched by human hand or disgraced with dust.

"Who are you?" demanded a tall, fat, blond woman who did not resemble the Disney-esque hag Reg had been expecting. She had on a pink apron that clashed with whatever she was wearing underneath, something red and flowery and not Reg's style at all.

"Hi... I'm looking for Smaranda Firea," Reg explained.

"I didn't ask who you're looking for. I asked who you are. Don't you know the answer?"

"Well... yes. I know the answer. I'm Reg Rawlins. I'm a psychic from..."

The woman waved away any details. "Why are you here? You could not get in without an invitation. And that means you spoke to my homunculus."

"Homunculus?" Reg repeated.

"The creature I created," she motioned to the door, even though Reg was sure that the boy had not gone back out the door. "The child who brought you?"

"You created him?" Reg shook her head. "That's crazy. You can't create a person. I mean, not like… making him instead of birthing him. You can't just create something out of nothing."

"Out of nothing, no," Sma agreed. "The seed of the sun and the moon, nurtured and grown, warmed by secret fire." She raised her brows. "It's not like you can buy a kit on Amazon."

Reg looked around. "I don't think Amazon delivers here."

Sma chuckled. "Sadly, no. I have to pick deliveries up in town. Which means I have to deal with people. Like you."

"You'd rather not have anything to do with people?"

"Exactly. People will just irritate you, offend you, and stab you in the back. They are all out to look after their own interests and don't care how it affects anyone else. Why would I want anything to do with anyone like that?"

"Well… you have to put up with the idiots so that you can have a chance of meeting the others. The good ones."

"The good ones?" Sma repeated. She looked toward Corvin and Marta. "Is this your example of the good ones? Some has-been warlock and a cop who doesn't have a clue what this is all about?"

"Uh… that's not very fair. You don't know anything about any of us."

"I know you're here to bother me when I haven't done anything to you. You think you can force your way into my house without my permission to see and do whatever you like. Why do you think I live way out here? Why do you think I have so many safeguards in place? And still, even with all of that, you still find a way to blunder your way through all of the roadblocks to show up on my doorstep."

"We came to talk to you about the truffles." Reg tried to remain focused on their true mission and not get sidetracked by Sma. She had her own grievances. But they were not Reg's problem and she couldn't let them take over.

CHAPTER FORTY-FOUR

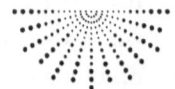

What truffles?"

"The truffles that you are distributing through your Tennessee company."

"What would I have to do with any company in Tennessee? That's ridiculous. Everybody knows I only leave my house when I have to, when I can't find anyone else to help me pick up my deliveries in town or run other errands. Why would I go to Tennessee?"

"I don't think you went to Tennessee. I think that you created a company there to divert people's attention. To make them think that you were just distributing the truffles for some corporation, not making them yourself."

"You don't know anything."

"What I don't understand is *why* you did it," Reg said. "I don't get why you would try to poison people or to affect their behavior. If you live out here and don't have anything to do with anyone else, what grudge do you have against the people who live in town?"

"You don't know anything about it. If they stayed in town, that would be one thing, but they don't. They come out here. They say they need to make the town bigger, the highway wider. They have to take my land because they want more people to move into town.

Why would we need more people to live in town? Why would we want the town to encroach on our land?"

"There are legal processes to express your objections," Marta inserted. "There are ways to make your wishes and arguments known."

"And they still take it," Sma shouted. "It doesn't matter if you object or not. If we *all* object," she made a motion that included her neighbors, "they will *still* take our land. What kind of legal process is that?"

"The Town Council hears the arguments on both sides, and others who have an opinion on it can tell how they feel, and then when the council has weighed the pros and cons, the needs of the community, then they come to a balanced decision…"

"And people like me get their land taken away," Sma screeched. "My family has owned this land for centuries. We tamed it when there was no one here. Made a place for ourselves and our children, and our children's children. And the town can just walk in and take it away because they think it is a better idea?"

Jessup bit her lip. There wasn't much she could say when the democratic process had apparently already taken place and the municipality had decided to expropriate the land. Land that they would only pay pennies on the dollar for, even though Sma's family had lived there for generations.

Reg had to admit it didn't sound very fair.

"Maybe there is somewhere you can appeal," she suggested. "It's not necessarily over."

"They are coming with bulldozers. Does that sound like they are willing to talk anymore? Like they are willing to wait on the development one more time?"

"Well…" Reg tried to pull it all together in her head in a way that made sense. She saw the bulldozers in her mind, coming to knock down the beautiful old house and all of its contents. "It's unfair. But…" she shook her head, "I don't see how poisoning everyone in town will help anything."

"I'm not poisoning everyone in town," Sma objected. She

motioned Reg farther into the room. "Sit down. Why are you still standing there?"

Reg looked back at Corvin and Marta, and they nodded, agreeing that Reg should obey. Reg couldn't help feeling a little like Hansel and Gretel, who should not have gone into the witch's house. That had been a bad idea, and Reg didn't think sitting down to talk to the witch would help matters.

But she sat down anyway in a chair that looked like it belonged in some king's dressing room rather than under Reg's behind.

Marta and Corvin moved forward but didn't sit down. Sma did not invite them to. They stood to Reg's side and slightly behind her, as if she were protecting them. But she was not.

"I can understand you being mad," she told Sma. "I would be too. But you're poisoning a lot of innocent people. None of the people who have died had anything to do with the town taking your land."

"Sometimes people get in the way of progress," Sma said without concern. "At least, that's what they told me. If you get in the way of progress... things can happen. It's too bad, but... progress needs to... move forward. And those who try to stop it will get run over."

"An old lady? A teenage girl trying to find her place in life? A little boy? How are they standing in the way of your progress? None of them were doing anything to hurt you."

"I'm not the one who decides who gets in the way. Those people were not targeted. They were just bystanders. It may be sad, but I didn't choose for them to eat the truffles or to get hurt."

"You distributed truffles all over Black Sands. Made sure that everyone got some. Offered them as free samples and made them addictive so people would keep buying them. Until they died."

"You see?" Sma raised her hands palms-up. "I didn't target those people. Everybody had the choice to eat them or not. They chose to... and I can't help what happened next."

"You couldn't control what happened next?"

"I didn't target those people. Only... one person was supposed to die."

Reg swallowed hard and thought about all of the people they had interviewed. Those poor families who, even if they couldn't feel the full weight of their grief because of the addicting truffles, had still lost loved ones for no reason. Plucked out of their lives because of a fight over land they didn't even know existed.

"Who was supposed to die?"

"The mayor. He's the one who let this happen and wouldn't step in to change anything. He is the one who should suffer the consequences of his actions."

"The mayor?"

As far as Reg knew, he hadn't even been sick.

Marta held up a hand. "Wait, the mayor? I thought the two of you were related somehow."

"Yes," Sma agreed serenely. "That is how I was able to target him. By targeting his blood. If he eats the truffles, enough of them, then he will die."

"The blood you share," Reg said. "You were distantly related, so you targeted your own blood, knowing that he shared enough of it for the truffles to kill him."

"And the other people who died?" Corvin asked.

Sma shrugged. "They must share my blood as well. Ancient families… they all mix at some point. There may be others yet too. If they continue to eat the truffles, they will die."

"The mayor's wife has him on a diet," Marta said. "He's probably one of the only people in town who *isn't* eating the truffles right now. Aside from you two," she looked at Corvin and Reg as if they had done something wrong.

Sma considered this. "That's unfortunate." She ran her fingers through her blond locks. "When he was younger, chocolate truffles were one of his favorite treats."

"So you made truffles and put a spell on them so that they would poison someone of your blood who ate them. And spread them all over town so the mayor couldn't miss them. You figured he would eat enough of the truffles to kill him."

Sma nodded her agreement. "Maybe that would stop the bulldozers."

"Not likely," Corvin disagreed. "Chances are, it wouldn't slow down or stop any development. It doesn't all hinge on the mayor and what he says. There are lots of other people and committees involved. And once the process is started, one person's death won't make that much difference."

"At least I will know, when the bulldozers come, that he is dead."

Except that he wasn't. As far as they all knew, the mayor wasn't even eating the truffles, unless he sneaked a couple behind his wife's back. He would probably be just fine and, instead, innocent bystanders would be buried.

"You don't care at all about the people who are dead?" she demanded.

"No. The truffles… dull the emotions. No one will feel too badly about it."

"Their families still care that they died! They will still mourn. And it won't make any sense to them that you just wanted to kill off anyone related to you."

"Just the mayor. I knew other people might die too. People who were frail or had other illnesses. But that's just something I had to be prepared for. As it turned out, it didn't bother me too much."

Reg turned her head to look at Marta, mentally encouraging her to make an arrest.

Marta shook her head.

"What?" Reg demanded in a whisper.

Marta leaned forward, so she was hovering right over Reg. "I don't have enough for an arrest right now. Just a random confession. I'll need something back from the autopsies. And lab tests showing that the truffles were poisoned. If they really were. And if it was magical instead of chemical…" Marta shook her head. "That will need to be dealt with by another authority. Not the police."

"She murdered those people."

"The courts won't charge on a magical curse. Not anymore. That ended centuries ago. Now it is up to practitioners to take care of it themselves. The covens and the other regulators."

"Then get someone out here who can deal with her. She's guilty! You heard her say so. You need to arrest her."

"It isn't as easy as that. And it will take time. It's not going to happen today, Reg."

Reg shook her head impatiently. She hated bureaucracy.

"Quit whispering," Sma told them. "It's rude." She moved into the kitchen they could see through an open doorway. "Can I offer you any tea? Truffles?"

Reg looked at Corvin and saw full agreement in his face. There was no way they were going to have tea with the witch.

At Reg's polite "No, thank you," Sma cackled.

CHAPTER FORTY-FIVE

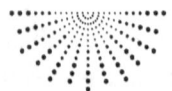

*A*t least getting back home was easier than finding Sma's gingerbread house in the woods. Reg was tired out, both emotionally and physically. She wanted to do something that made a difference. She had thought that once they found Sma and established that she had been the poisoner, whether accidental or intentional, they would be able to stop the poisonings, and Sma would be behind bars or magically bound in some way. But Marta refused to arrest her under the non-magical laws, since they could not prove that there was any dangerous foreign substance in the truffles. Corvin had refused to bind her or do anything magical to ensure that she could not make or distribute any more truffles.

"I don't have any authority over Sma," he told her gravely as Reg once more knelt beside the burbling waterfall to quench her thirst. "I only have authority over my own coven and, even then, I am limited in the disciplinary measures I can take. I can't invoke shunning or have someone expelled from the coven without a tribunal. I can only give a verbal or written reprimand or lay their offenses before the coven. Any more than that…" He shrugged. "That's the limit of my authority. And for someone like Sma, who is not in my coven, all I can do is report her to the regulators. Like Marta says, it will take some time for them to consider the case, convene a tribunal, and decide what to do with her. These things never move very quickly."

Reg sat back on her feet, wiping moisture from her face. Corvin was standing a distance from her, downwind, so she wouldn't be distracted by his scent. She appreciated that he thought enough like a predator to do it automatically.

"So she gets to just stay there and keep doing what she's doing?" Reg challenged. "Killing more people? She doesn't even care that there is collateral damage. As long as she gets what it is that she wants."

"I'll deal with the truffles," Marta said. "I'll report our suspicions that they are poisoned before we get any of the lab tests back and pressure the authorities to have them recalled until it can be established that they are safe. Sma would have to jump through a lot of hoops to get them back into distribution after a forced recall, and I don't think she's the type of person that would do that."

"So no more truffles."

"No."

"But what about the bags that are already out there? A lot of people have bought them and still have them in their cupboards." Reg thought about Sarah. Did she have any more left? If she ran out, would she go to Reg's cottage to retrieve the bag she had given Reg?

"The recall will ask for them to be returned to the store where they bought them."

"Not everyone will return them. They might finish the rest of what they have. The first few didn't poison them, so they think they are fine."

"We can't control everyone. We will do what we can to get them out of people's homes, but it won't be easy. Not when they're so addictive."

They started back toward the car. Marta had dropped a pin on her phone to save its location, and Reg hoped that the modern technology would work better to find the car than it had to find the house. But no one had magically hidden the car. Reg looked around and didn't see the homunculus anywhere. Apparently, he didn't stop people from leaving, only kept trespassers from approaching.

What would he have done if they had tried to force their way past him? He was small and, although Reg knew from experience that small creatures like pixies could be inhumanly strong, she wasn't sure the diminutive boy would have been able to hold all three of them back.

But who knew what other traps there might have been or if he would have turned into something else that was more threatening or more capable of keeping them away.

"What exactly is a homunculus?"

"I don't know if they actually exist," Marta offered. "He just looked like a normal boy to me. I think Sma was just gaslighting us, saying he was a homunculus."

"But what is one?"

"It is a sort of… a mini person that can be created using alchemy," Corvin explained, choosing his words carefully. "Like most alchemical creations or processes, it's hard to know whether they are really possible. Whether someone once created them or just imagined it could be done or told stories about having done it when they had not. Alchemy was as much about the lore as it was actually being able to do the things the proponents claimed were possible—turning lead into gold, creating a stone or elixir that prolongs life indefinitely, creating a homunculus…"

"Do you think it was a real homunculus?"

He shook his head. "I don't know. Just because I've never seen one, that doesn't mean it wasn't. Whether it was a natural child or something created by the witch, it did seem to be… enchanted. Not a child who had just been given instructions to keep any strangers away from the house."

Reg nodded and shuddered.

She kept a close watch on Marta and the GPS as they worked their way back toward the car, alert for any sign that they were being pulled off course by some kind of confusion or camouflage spell. For a while, she was aware of a crow fluttering from branch to branch overhead. Not leading them this time, but maybe keeping an eye on things to make sure that they would be able to get back.

Eventually, they came into view of the car, and all breathed a sigh of relief that it was still there and they hadn't been cursed to wander Sma's woods forevermore.

* * *

After getting up early two days in a row, Reg expected to pass out again like the night before, her body dictating that she needed the extra sleep whether her brain agreed or not. But instead, the opposite occurred.

Reg's brain was working so hard to review everything that had happened at Sma's house and everything she had said and that they had been able to confirm. Around and around like a hamster wheel, never getting to the end where she could finally rest. Instead of being exhausted, her body was restless and she found herself pacing around the house, trying to settle herself down enough to be able to sleep.

She couldn't stop thinking about the Shoops and their children. About the many other families and children in Black Sands who had truffles in their cupboards. She was worried that there would be further deaths as people continued to eat what they had purchased instead of returning them to the store where they had bought them. They were so addictive, people wouldn't want to give them up. And since the poison seemed to take several days to work, others might have already eaten too many of them and, like a time bomb, the countdown to their deaths was already ticking.

After pacing up and down the cottage for some time, Reg crossed the yard to the big house and let herself into Sarah's kitchen. She didn't knock or call out. The house was silent. Reg found a partial bag of truffles in the cupboard and shoved them into one of the capacious pockets of her skirt, out of sight.

She crept up the stairs and along the hallway until she found Sarah's bedroom. She stood outside the door, ear pressed to the crack, until she could hear Sarah's raspy breathing. Reg stood there for a long time before returning to the guest cottage, where she got rid of her bag of truffles and the half-filled bag of truffles from Sarah's house permanently. Being able to transport objects over distances had its advantages.

The effort of disposing of the truffles left her tired. Reg fell asleep on the couch and, when she woke up, she could not remember the moment she had sat down and closed her eyes and rested her head.

She had a crick in her neck. She rubbed it and tried to work out the knot while her coffee brewed. She didn't want to walk around with her neck cocked to the side all day or unable to turn her head all the way in both directions. She hated that.

She watched her phone screen, tapping through several news alerts and video streamers she liked to watch before seeing a press appearance by the Black Sands mayor earlier that morning.

He had on a serious face and spoke in a grave voice, giving the residents of Black Sands a sobering account of the fact that the distribution of the truffles was rumored to have been a plot against him personally, but also against all residents of Black Sands, by an emotionally disturbed individual who wanted to do as much damage as possible to those around her.

He sternly repeated several times that even if the residents of Black Sands believed that the truffles they had purchased and had already begun eating were safe and uncontaminated, they should be destroyed or turned in immediately, and that the poison might be delayed by several days. The mayor did not tell everyone who had eaten the truffles to go to the hospital immediately for investigation and treatment, which would have resulted in the hospital being completely overwhelmed. But he did advise that they carefully watch for any poisoning symptoms and pay extra attention to friends and neighbors without families to ensure that anyone who seemed sick could get immediate treatment.

What would the hospital do when these people complained about vague poisoning symptoms? Reg had no idea. Could anything actually be done for them?

The phone rang, interrupting a question-and-answer session

following the mayor's announcement. It was Marta. Reg hit the speaker button.

"Hi. I was just watching the mayor."

"Yeah, he did a pretty good job, I thought. Serious, but not inciting a panic."

"The hospital is going to be busy."

"Yeah, all of the hypochondriacs should be heading over there right now, and it's going to be harder to get rid of them than convincing people that antibiotics can't cure their cold symptoms. But... I don't know what else to suggest. We don't want people to ignore symptoms in themselves or their loved ones if they prevent more deaths before everyone gets the toxin or spell out of their system."

"If it is a spell, then will it ever really go away? Or will they eventually die from the curse?"

"A curse like that, especially one that has been spread so thinly over the entire population of Black Sands, takes a lot of energy to uphold for any length of time. Curses don't last forever, despite what you might have heard about Egyptian mummies. I think that this one will only last a few days. And then... such things are also affected by the demise of the spellcaster."

"Right. Wait—what?"

"The demolition was supposed to start today. The police department sent officers over with the heavy equipment to provide security and ensure they weren't attacked by the residents whose land had been appropriated."

"Yeah?"

"Well... they had no trouble finding the gingerbread house, and there was no homunculus guarding it this time. Everything was very... normal."

"She left?" Reg demanded, a lump in her throat. She *knew* they shouldn't have left Sma there alone. She understood what Corvin and Marta had said about their hands being tied, but there must have been *something* they could have done to prevent her from running away. They should have seen it. There was nothing to stop her from leaving. The homunculus had said she didn't have any attachments. The neighbors had made that clear. Sma herself had shown that she didn't care about anyone in town, even if they were her blood relatives.

They should have done something to stop her. There must have been something they could have done.

"She left... permanently," Marta said.

Of course she had taken all of her important possessions with her. She knew she was going to lose her house. She had exhausted all other options. Maybe that was why her house had been so sparsely furnished. She had already packed the rest off somewhere. Maybe she had another house in another town waiting for her. Or off in the wilderness somewhere where nobody would be able to find her.

"You have to look for her," Reg insisted. "You have to do it right away, while there is still a warm trail. This is the best time to be able to track her down again. Once the trail goes cold..."

"We don't need to track her down, Reg," Marta said patiently. "She's dead."

"Dead?"

"The victim of her own truffles, it looks like. They *were* targeted against people who shared her blood."

"Including herself."

"Apparently, yeah. I guess she knew she wouldn't be able to do anything to stop the appropriation. So... she had another way out."

"Oh."

Maybe that was part of the reason Sma hadn't shown any emotion over the other deaths. She had already been eating the truffles. They were people she was not close to and, with the effects of the truffles, she didn't have to feel any grief or sadness for them.

Maybe that had been the plan from the start.

CHAPTER FORTY-SIX

*R*eg was enjoying a meal with Marta at The Crystal Bowl.
Things had returned to normal, so it seemed like it had
been a long time since she had been worried about the truffles and
their quest to stop the poisonings of the Black Sands magical
community.

It seemed like something she had only dreamt. Around her,
people were returning to normal. When she had asked Marta about
having dinner with both her and Corvin, Marta had immediately
declined.

"I'm not having anything to do with Corvin," she insisted.
"Just because I cooperated with him this once, that doesn't mean it
will happen again. I don't want to be anywhere near him."

It soothed Reg for things to be back to normal. The ceasefire
between Marta and Corvin had not been comfortable. It had been
an itching, burning bramble that made her worry just what was
coming next. Especially when she had discovered that the changed
emotions and behavior in the people around her could be a
precursor to death. What if Marta Jessup had been a distant rela-
tion to Sma? Had she eaten enough of the truffles to have been
killed by them?

Marta raised her glass. "To Reg Rawlins, hero of Black Sands."

"Hero?" Reg asked skeptically. No one was calling her that. Though it was true that she had received a call from the mayor. A personal call from the mayor, even if it had been put through by an administrative assistant for him. A personal call where he had thanked her for her part in unraveling the mystery and identifying Sma as the source of the tainted truffles.

"I could have been killed," he told Reg solemnly. "I didn't have very many of those truffles, but I certainly could have snuck a few more, and then..." She could picture the big man ponderously shaking his head, as she had seen him do on news reels. "Well, let me just thank you personally, young lady, for your part in figuring out where this plague was coming from and saving the lives of an untold number of residents, one of whom was me."

"Well... thank you," Reg had told him in embarrassment. How could she tell him that it hadn't been anything to do with his safety? There were few things she cared less about than politics and the welfare of politicians, no matter how good they appeared to be. "I'm glad that no one else was killed."

That part was true, anyway.

"You saved a whole town. How could you not be a hero?" Marta challenged.

"I didn't save the whole town. Only a small percentage would have been killed. And even if I had saved everyone, it wasn't all me. You were there. Corvin. I couldn't have done it without either of you. I wasn't even the one who figured out that something was wrong. That was Corvin."

"Nevertheless... You *are* a hero. And real heroes never think that they are. They think they just did what anyone else would have done."

Reg had opened her mouth to make just that objection, and closed it again. Marta smirked and took a sip of her wine.

A woman approached the table, clutching her purse in front of her. Clearly not a waitress or other staff member. She looked nervous, scared to death about approaching Reg.

Reg smiled encouragingly. Whatever this woman was worried about, she didn't have any reason to fear Reg.

"You're Reg Rawlins?" the woman asked. Her eyes darted to Marta, then back to Reg. "The psychic? The person who got the Mystical Morsels recalled?"

Reg nodded cautiously. "Yes. That was me."

"You should be ashamed of yourself!" The woman thunked her heavy handbag down on the table, sending everything wobbling and shaking. Reg barely pulled back her fingers in time to avoid having them crushed.

She stared at the woman. "What?"

"Those truffles were the only thing in my life that I could be happy about! What kind of person goes around taking truffles away from people? Tell me that!"

"They were... tainted," Reg said faintly. She didn't know what else to say. Surely anyone who had heard her name on the news had heard the part about the truffles being poisoned. "I couldn't... just let people keep eating them."

"They were the highlight of my life! They were so delicious, so smooth and creamy. And now there are no more of them. They're all gone. Every last one of them." She shook her head. "How could you do that to me?"

"I'm sorry," Reg tried. Even though, of course, she wasn't sorry. If the woman resented not being poisoned, there wasn't much Reg could do about that. "But they were causing a lot of issues. The way people felt and treated each other. The deaths. A little boy was killed, and I'm sure you understand that I couldn't stand by and see other children killed."

"So stop the children from eating them. But I am a grown adult. I can decide what I want to do with my own body. I shouldn't have to give something up that is perfectly legal. They were harmless. I heard that that witch wasn't even killed by the truffles. There was a conspiracy, and when the mayor and his people got there—"

"The mayor wasn't there," Marta interrupted. "He was sitting on his fat behind at his desk. He didn't want to have to lose his precious truffles either. But I was there, and I can tell you there wasn't any conspiracy. There was no answer at the door, so we effected entry, and that was when we found Sma Firea dead. She knew the truffles would kill her. She's the one who made that happen. No one else. Not the mayor, not me, and not Reg."

"The truffles were not dangerous to healthy adults—"

"When did you finish yours?" Marta interrupted.

"What are you talking about? They were recalled a week ago—"

"But you didn't turn yours in. When did you finish them?"

The woman's eyes burned in her pale face. "Yesterday."

"And today, you're in withdrawal. You feel like crap. Because of the addictive stuff Firea put into the truffles. In a few days, you won't feel so bad, and you'll be able to see that Reg did the right thing."

The woman shook her head. "I'll never forgive you for what you did here."

"Move along, now," Marta instructed. "You're finished here."

The woman's nostrils flared, but Marta continued to stare her in the eye until the woman looked away, finally backing down. She lifted her heavy purse again and, after giving Reg one last scowl, she walked away.

EPILOGUE

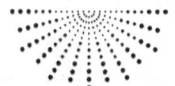

The way approaching Sma's gingerbread house was fenced off with construction barriers and warning signs that threatened death, or something close to it, if people trespassed on the property the municipality had appropriated.

But there were many ways over, through, or past physical barriers, and the signs didn't scare Reg. She drank again from the pool below the waterfall and approached the house. If they were going to knock it down, they had not yet done so. Maybe they hadn't appropriated the part of the property the house was on, or perhaps it had historical significance that kept them from knocking it down, or the town planned to use it as a visitor center or administrative building. At any rate, she was happy to see it was still standing.

She started walking across the clearing toward the house and, in a few moments, was faced by the homunculus.

"You have not been invited."

Or maybe the homunculus had stopped anyone from knocking the house down.

"I was invited," Reg told him. "Don't you remember me? Remember how we talked about the truffles and how they are to die for?"

The words didn't seem to have the same impact as the last time Reg had been there. But there was still a subtle reaction.

"The truffles are gone," the boy said sadly.

"I know. But they were bad for people. So really, that's a good thing."

"Why did you return?"

"I couldn't stop thinking about you. And about Sma, making those truffles… and then dying here."

"It was her ancestral home."

"Yes," Reg agreed. "That kind of thing can have quite a hold over some people."

"She could never leave here." The homunculus folded his arms and looked around.

"Does that mean that you are tied to this place?"

The boy's flat, black eyes stared at her. He didn't blink. She wasn't sure what they reminded her of. A fish? A shark? But she didn't find him threatening and, even though she could feel no emotions from him, she didn't think he was without feelings. There was a certain poignancy to his still being there after his creator had died.

"Yes," he said finally. "As long as Sma is here, so am I."

"Didn't they take her away?"

"Only her outer form."

"I could talk to her ghost. See if I could get her to release you."

"There is no release. Without her, I cannot exist."

"Because she created you?"

He nodded. "A homunculus has no will of its own."

"Don't you, though? Here you are, after she is gone. Speaking and acting for yourself. You are… self-aware. Not just an extension of her."

"Such a thing is not possible."

"But… it is."

He said nothing. And she hadn't asked a question, so how could he give her an answer to her unspoken thoughts?

"You can't leave here?"

He shook his head.

"What if… I found a way. Would you want to go somewhere else?"

"Where would that be?" he asked tentatively.

"I don't know. Another house. Somewhere in the forest where you could be happier. Somewhere you could make friends."

"A homunculus has no free will."

"And if I could find a way to free you?"

He just stared at her with his slate black eyes.

Did you enjoy this book? Reviews and recommendations are vital to making a book successful.

Please leave a review at your favorite book store or review site and share it with your friends.

Don't miss the following bonus material:
Sign up for mailing list to get a free ebook
Read a sneak preview chapter
Other books by P.D. Workman
Learn more about the author

DON'T MISS A THING! GET THE LATEST NEWS AND A FREE EBOOK

Your First Taste

PDWORKMAN.COM/SIGNUP

PREVIEW OF LUNAR LIES

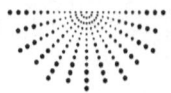

Lunar Lies is book #21 in the Reg Rawlins Psychic Investigator series.

Reg thought she had left her past behind, but when her former lover shows up in town with a dangerous secret, she must confront the truth of her past and act.

PREVIEW CHAPTER 1

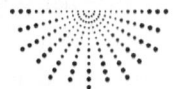

*M*alcolm Witchell was Reg's first appointment of the evening. She had not met with him before, so she wasn't sure what to expect.

He was an older man with a round, stout figure and gray hair. He seemed pleasant enough when she met him at the door, but she could see a dark aura around him when she had him sit down on the wicker couch in the living room. The smiles and friendly manner hid what he was really feeling. Of course, that was not unusual. Society demanded that people hide their negative feelings and put on a show for the outside world. That was true even in Black Sands, where there was such a high population of psychics and other magical practitioners that a person couldn't hide his true feelings for long unless he was skilled at blocking such intrusions.

"So, what can I do for you today, Mr. Witchell? Was there a particular type of reading you were hoping to have? A decision you're trying to make or something you're trying to reconcile from the past?"

"I was told you're very good with the crystal ball."

Reg nodded. "Sure. No problem." She retrieved her crystal from its place on the shelf and put it on the coffee table in front of the wicker couch. She sat down next to him. Close enough to feel the cold, anxious cloud that enveloped him. He was troubled about something. But that didn't come as a surprise. Many of her clients were going through a difficult time and needed someone to help them through it.

Reg gathered her thin red box braids together in both hands and pushed them back behind her shoulders. She adjusted the scarf around her head and closed her eyes. She just sat there quietly for a moment. Witchell shifted beside her, unable to stay still. He was uncomfortable in his own skin. Maybe second-guessing his decision to come to her. Too many negative emotions might block her from being able to do a successful reading.

"Can I get you a cup of tea, Mr. Witchell? Something to help you to relax?"

"I wouldn't turn down a glass of Scotch."

Reg smiled. "I can give you one… but alcohol can mess up a reading. It's not the best idea. If tea would do…"

He cleared his throat and shrugged. "I supposed. Can't hurt anything, can it?"

Reg stood back up to make the tea. While she was in the kitchen area of the front room, Starlight jumped down from the windowsill in the bedroom and came out to see who was there with Reg. She bent down to scratch the black and white tuxedo cat's ears.

"Do you want to help me with the reading today?"

He purred and nuzzled her and wound around her legs.

"Do you mind cats, Mr. Witchell? Starlight is quite a powerful psychic himself and helps to magnify my gifts. If you don't mind him taking part in the reading…"

"I like cats just fine." Witchell patted his ample lap. "Come here, kitty."

Starlight put back his ears and looked at Reg in alarm. She sent him reassuring vibes. "He'll probably sit with me for it. If he wants to participate."

Witchell grunted. He watched Reg get the tea ready. In a few minutes, Reg sat back down with him, a cup of tea for each of them on the tray she set on the coffee table.

"Why don't you tell me what you're hoping to get from today's reading," she suggested. "Is there a particular question that you have in mind? Something that is troubling you?"

He looked her over, eyes bright and piercing. "I have certain concerns," he said slowly. "But if I tell them to you ahead of time…"

"Then you can't be sure whether I'm really exercising psychic powers or just telling you what you want to hear?"

He looked a little relieved at her suggestion, smiling tentatively. "Yes. I suppose that's insulting, but…"

Reg sipped her tea. "Not at all. When people come for a reading, they are usually looking for evidence that I really am psychic and not just putting on a show. They want to believe, and they need help, but if they just want friendly advice, they could go to a friend. Or a bartender or therapist."

"Yes, that's right."

Reg didn't tell him she'd been a pretty convincing psychic even before discovering that she had actual psychic powers. People who wanted desperately to believe were easy to con.

"That's just fine." Reg nodded. "You don't need to tell me anything about what you hope to hear tonight. Though if I don't have specific directions as to what you are looking for, the results might be unexpected. You may get advice on matters other than what you came for today. The fates aren't always cooperative."

He shrugged, but his hooded eyes told her he took her caution as a sign that she wasn't really psychic and he might not get what he had come for.

She put her teacup down and turned her attention to the crystal ball. Starlight approached and jumped up on the couch. He squeezed himself against Reg's leg, keeping her between him and the client. Why didn't cats ever want attention from the people most willing to give it to them?

Reg rested her fingertips on the crystal and looked past the shiny surface reflections, focusing on the inner depths. She thought about the man sitting next to her, reaching out all her senses to gather what she could about him. His emotions, his discomfort with being there, his anxiety… over seeing her? Over something else that was going on in his life?

Starlight added his strength to Reg's, helping to sharpen and clarify the feelings.

Yes, he was anxious and uncomfortable. Something to do with his personal life? His business? Family?

She could see shapes within the crystal, but they were still unclear.

"You are very anxious about the future," Reg said slowly. "You are seeking direction, unsure of your choices…"

He tensed slightly. Wrong step. Reg backtracked.

"You have made a decision already. But you're not sure."

That felt more correct. Reg explored this, trying to put herself into his mind, to see him in the crystal ball and discover what choice he had made and why he was so concerned about it.

She saw him moving among shelves, the images very dark and fuzzy still. Shelves of what? Shelves in a storage room? Had he put something away and then forgotten where he had left it? People often came to her to look for lost objects.

But that wasn't it. He had come to her about a decision, and if it was something to do with the shelves, it wasn't hide and seek. She looked at the world from his perspective within the crystal, standing in the middle and turning to look all around him, three hundred and sixty degrees.

It was not a basement storage room; it was a store. A small store with dim light coming in through the front windows. Before opening or after closing, no one else in the store, and the main lights not turned on.

Reg studied the shelves, frowning. A toy store?

The products on the shelves were old. Or old-fashioned, anyway. Carved wooden cars and trucks. Sets of small animals. A blocky toddler puzzle. A turtle with wheels that looked like its flippers moved when it was pulled by a string.

"Is it about the toy store?" Reg asked.

Witchell took in a sharp breath. She didn't look at him, keeping her eyes on the image within the crystal.

He still wasn't sure whether he should tell her anything about the questions he had come to her with. Reg didn't press him, but continued to observe the images within the crystal.

"It's very nice. I'll bet grandparents especially like to buy the kinds of toys for their grandkids that they played with themselves."

Witchell grunted. "Yes."

But he wasn't happy about that. Why not? It must be fulfilling to craft the little toys, to make something with his hands that was so beautiful and practical and would be enjoyed for many years and passed down from one child to the next generation.

But he wasn't the one making the toys, or didn't enjoy it. He was dissatisfied, looking for something else to do. Maybe the business was not doing well. Maybe people didn't buy many wooden toys anymore and his business was foundering. Looking for a new direction.

"Yes," Reg murmured, as much to herself and Starlight as to Witchell. "It isn't working anymore. The old ways aren't always the best. People aren't buying quality wooden toys anymore. Not many of them, anyway."

"It's a dying market," Witchell confirmed, the words popping out of him like a released cork. Something that he hadn't intended to tell her, but her words had freed him to talk about it. "If we don't adapt, we will have to close the business."

"You and your partner," Reg said, seeing another man in the picture, smiling and talking to a customer about the process of lovingly crafting each piece. How each was unique and made individually, not mass-produced. There were no robots, no assembly line, just careful, loving hands. "Your brother?"

"My uncle," Witchell corrected. "But... we grew up together. We are like brothers."

In the crystal ball, the customer smiled and left the store without putting in an order or purchasing one of the completed toys off the shelf. The uncle's face fell, and he shook his head. He'd thought that the woman would buy a toy. Maybe several. She'd seemed like a promising prospect. But she had left without buying a thing.

"Are the two of you trying to figure out what to do with the business?" Reg asked. "How to keep your customers or get more?"

"I know what we need to do," Witchell said. His aura grew darker. "We have to change with the times. No one wants to buy that kind of thing anymore. Maybe we could still keep a few, a shelf in the back of the store where we sell old fashioned toys to the oldsters. Sentimental fools who remember what it was like to play with them and want to relive their own childhoods. Because kids don't want that anymore. They don't want old-fashioned wooden toys."

The world was now full of lights and sirens, screens that could play dozens of games and keep children occupied all day. Toys that talked and beeped and moved, that came with apps and movies and were backed by huge advertising dollars.

"What does your uncle think of that?"

"Arch is too old-fashioned. He just doesn't see it. He thinks it is just a temporary lull. That the pendulum is bound to swing the other way and people will come back to the old toys. It isn't a pendulum. That stuff is in the past. No one is going back there. The world is moving forward."

Reg nodded. In the crystal, she saw Arch's face, wistful and a little hurt. Witchell didn't want to see him sad. But he couldn't hold out and not do anything to change their business model, either. Ignoring the problem wouldn't make it go away.

Reg was mindful of Witchell's dark aura. He'd already made a decision, and he hated it. He felt like there wasn't any other option.

"What are you going to do?"

"I'm sending him on vacation. A well-deserved break, so that when he comes back, he will be rested and rejuvenated."

But that wasn't the whole story. That was just what he was telling Arch.

"And while he's gone... I'm going to make some changes."

PREVIEW CHAPTER 2

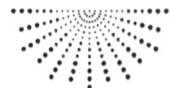

*R*eg was still looking into the crystal ball. She saw nothing but swirling darkness for a moment, and then... destruction. The toy store was gutted, everything removed from the shelves and all the shelving units and furniture torn out. Soft lighting replaced by bright fluorescent lights. A long, brushed steel counter and fresh new shelving and display units. Filled with brain candy. Electronic devices of all sorts, big brand toys, all of the popular stuff. Spic and span and shiny new.

Was that really what Witchell wanted? The wholesale destruction of what his family had built together? He said they would still sell the old toys at the back of the store, but Reg didn't see any place left for them. Trash bags of handmade toys were disposed of in big garbage bins. Nothing was left of Uncle Arch or what he had built.

And that was what Witchell wanted him to come home to?

The man would die. With his life's work destroyed and trashed, what reason was there for him to go on? Malcolm Witchell would be sad, but it would free him to run the toy store however he pleased, without anyone else telling him what he had to do or not do.

And then what? The renovation of the toy store would cost

money. Would he be able to recoup that? Would he be able to turn a profit? Or would the change mean the end of the store?

"You would… do all of this while he was gone?" she asked Witchell.

"It needs to be done. It's the only way we will be able to recover and run the store profitably. I know that Arch won't like it, that's why I'm going to do it while he is gone. Then there isn't a fight over it. It's just done."

"You don't think he'll be upset when he sees it?"

"Well, of course he'll be upset. For a little while. And then he'll see that it's turning a profit and that it means we can keep the store, when we wouldn't be able to if we just kept doing what we've been doing."

"And you're sure that a store like this—" Reg realized that he couldn't see what she had seen in the crystal, "—a modern store with all of the popular toy brands—will be able to turn a profit?"

"Well, they do, don't they?" He shook his head as if Reg was being stupid. "These are the things that the kids want. They go into the city to buy them. They'd rather buy them here than go all that way."

"I don't think…" Reg worded her statement carefully, "that lying to your business partner and making changes behind his back is going to work out the way you think it will. If you want to make changes, you need to talk to him."

"He just won't do it," Witchell insisted. "He won't want to make any changes. I already know that."

"This will not go well." Reg looked away from the crystal and leaned back. She looked him in the eye. "If you do this… it will destroy your relationship with your uncle."

"But without these changes, we won't have anything to live on. Things are already tight, too tight. We're putting money into the business instead of making it."

"If you replace all the wooden toys with popular modern stuff, won't you lose your current customers?"

He scowled at her. "They'll buy the new stuff."

"Will they?"

"If they don't, then new people will come. That's why we're getting the new stock."

Reg petted Starlight and scratched his ears. "I'm not sure what you wanted to ask me or what you were hoping to hear in this reading, but… if you want to know whether this is the right thing to do or not… I don't think it is. You need to be honest and transparent with your uncle. Tell him what the problems are and what you want to do. Because if you do this… send him away, and throw out all of the wooden toys, and make over the whole business… you'll lose him, and maybe the toy store too."

"That's not what I came to hear."

"No." Reg studied him. "But I think maybe you already knew. I think that's why you're feeling so… dark right now. You knew it was the wrong choice, but you were hoping I'd tell you to go ahead, that it was the only thing to do."

"I've already ordered supplies and started setting up contractors to do the work."

"Then you'd better stop them before they get too far. Tell them your financing didn't go through."

His expression was grim. "There is no financing. If this doesn't work, we're done."

"Talk to Arch. Otherwise… you're doomed to fail."

Lunar Lies, Book #21 of the *Reg Rawlins, Psychic Investigator series* by P.D. Workman
can be purchased at pdworkman.com

ABOUT THE AUTHOR

P.D. Workman is a USA Today Bestselling author, winner of several awards from Library Services for Youth in Custody and the InD'tale Magazine's Crowned Heart award, and has published over 100 mystery/suspense/thriller and young adult books, including stand alones and these series: Auntie Clem's Bakery cozy mysteries, Reg Rawlins Psychic Investigator paranormal mysteries, Zachary Goldman Mysteries (PI), Kenzie Kirsch Medical Thrillers, Parks Pat Mysteries (police procedural), and YA series: Tamara's Teardrops, Between the Cracks, and Breaking the Pattern.

Workman loves writing about the underdog, who the reader may love or hate. She has been praised for her realistic details, deep characterization, and sensitive handling of the serious social issues that appear in all of her stories, from light cozy mysteries through to darker, grittier young adult and mystery/suspense books.

> P. D. Workman, does not shy from probing the deep psychological scars of childhood trauma, mental illness, and addiction. Also characteristic of this author, these extremely sensitive issues are explored with extensive empathy, described with incredible clarity, and portrayed with profound insight.
>
> — —KIM, GOODREADS REVIEWER

Some of Workman's titles have been translated into Spanish, French, Portuguese, German, and Italian.

Workman began writing at an early age and is a prolific reader as well as writer. She is also passionate about teaching and learning, expresses her creativity through art and cooking, and loves exploring the Calgary parks and green spaces where the Parks Pat Mysteries are set. She was a legal assistant for many years and has done extensive charitable work.

Workman was born and raised in Alberta, Canada, and is married with one adult son.

* * *

Please visit P.D. Workman at pdworkman.com to see what else she is working on, to join her mailing list, and to link to her social networks.

* * *

If you enjoyed this book, please take the time to recommend it to other purchasers with a review or star rating and share it with your friends!

tiktok.com/@pdworkmanauthor

facebook.com/pdworkmanauthor

x.com/pdworkmanauthor

instagram.com/pdworkmanauthor

amazon.com/author/pdworkman

bookbub.com/authors/p-d-workman

goodreads.com/pdworkman

linkedin.com/in/pdworkman

pinterest.com/pdworkmanauthor

youtube.com/pdworkman

Find P.D. Workman's books at

PDWORKMAN.COM

Scan the QR code below